The Nightmare House

Sarah Allen

The Nightmare House

FARRAR STRAUS GIROUX

NEW YORK

Farrar Straus Giroux Books for Young Readers
An imprint of Macmillan Publishing Group, LLC
120 Broadway, New York, NY 10271 • mackids.com

Our books may be purchased in bulk for promotional, educational, or business use.
Please contact your local bookseller or the Macmillan Corporate and
Premium Sales Department at (800) 221-7945 ext. 5442 or by email at
MacmillanSpecialMarkets@macmillan.com.

Library of Congress Cataloging-in-Publication Data
Names: Allen, Sarah Elisabeth, author.
Title: The nightmare house / Sarah Allen.
Description: First edition. | New York : Farrar Straus Giroux, 2023. | Audience: Ages
10 to 12 | Audience: Grades 4–6 | Summary: "A middle-grade novel about a girl who
sees possessed souls and ventures into a haunted house in the forest on a mission to
save them, and defeat her own demons, in the process" —Provided by publisher.
Identifiers: LCCN 2022043068 | ISBN 9780374390952 (hardcover)
Subjects: CYAC: Haunted houses—Fiction. | Fear—Fiction. | Anxiety—Fiction. |
Friendship—Fiction. | Self-realization—Fiction. | LCGFT: Paranormal
fiction. | Psychological fiction. | Novels.
Classification: LCC PZ7.1.A4394 Ni 2023 | DDC [Fic]—dc23
LC record available at https://lccn.loc.gov/2022043068

First edition, 2023
Book design by Mallory Grigg
Printed in the United States of America by
Lakeside Book Company, Harrisonburg, Virginia

ISBN 978-0-374-39095-2
1 3 5 7 9 10 8 6 4 2

To C. S. Lewis, because I couldn't have written this without *The Screwtape Letters*. And to anyone who's ever met Fear— you're infinitely stronger than it wants you to know.

◆ ◆

But for one's health, as you say, it is
very necessary to work in the garden
and see the flowers growing.

—Vincent van Gogh

Monsters are real . . . They live inside
us, and sometimes, they win.

—Stephen King

The Nightmare House

Sunflowers

I saw a person with blank eyes today.

At first I thought it was the light, or maybe I'd just glimpsed something wrong out of the corner of my eye. I looked again. I looked closer.

Empty eyes. The baker had empty eyes. Blank like her irises weren't really a color, and that colorlessness had spread out into her eye sockets until they were caverns of nothing. Eyes I'd seen only in my nightmares. Many, many nightmares.

She was shelving loaves of bread, wiping down counters. She turned toward me and I couldn't help but look away.

I blinked tight. My brain had to be playing tricks. I gulped, then looked back a third time.

She was still looking at me.

With blank, white, nothing in her eyes.

I felt like someone was blowing arctic, icy wind through a straw down my spine, one shivering vertebra at a time.

Mom, do you see it? I asked. *Do you see her eyes?*

I wanted to run.

What about them, sweetie? Mom said, looking at the baker's face, then back at me.

You don't see it? I said.

See what? She seemed confused at my question. *What's wrong?* she said.

Mom paid for the red-velvet cupcakes, the ones we sometimes bring with us when we visit Grandma, and we left and went on our way as if nothing scary had happened, nothing strange at all.

Grandma gave me this spiral-bound notebook before she moved out of our house and into Olympus Assisted Living two months ago. She was the one I always talked to about the things I saw in my nightmares. The tall man. The growing house. The blank-eyed people.

I asked her what I was going to do after she left. Who was I going to talk to about what I saw in the night? She bought me this new, fresh notebook and told me to write about my fears. Put my nightmares and monsters in words and poems, because then, she said, at least some of them would be outside my head.

Now I'm seeing those blank eyes in real life. This couldn't have been what she meant.

Maybe it would have been easier to convince myself I was making a mistake, that my brain was playing tricks on me, if I hadn't seen blank, soulless eyes just like the baker's so, so many times since the nightmares started years ago.

Grandma said to write down my nightmares. Grandma, a poet, says words have power. She taught me about meter and enjambment and painting with words. I've been writing my nightmares in lines and verse like Grandma said, and maybe if I keep putting down the words, my notebook will help me make sense of whatever dreadful thing is going on. Mom didn't see the blank eyes. We were the only ones in the bakery: me,

Mom, and the baker who kept staring at me through white emptiness. I think Grandma was right, and writing down my nightmares will help me work out whether or not I'm just an eleven-year-old girl who's slowly losing her grip on reality. If nobody else sees the blank-eyed people, at least my notebook will know. My notebook with Van Gogh sunflowers on the cover will carry the nightmares.

And maybe they will finally, finally go away.

So it's up to you, sunflowers.

My name is Penny Hope. I am eleven years old and today I saw a person with blank, colorless eyes like a vacuum. And this time I wasn't dreaming.

Please help.

Soul-Sucked

I was seven the night the Fear Maker first came.

It was Halloween, and I didn't know that's who he was. Yet.

Green fabric paint still clung to my fingernails from the day before, when Mom and I had painted an old white pillowcase to be my trick-or-treat bag. Swirly-twirly painted pillowcases for Halloween, elaborate gingerbread houses with jelly-bean roofs for Christmas. That's what we did every year, Mom and me. Her fingertips were still paint-splattered, too.

Before that Halloween night, I was one kind of Penny.

The kind of Penny who could ride her bike without being afraid of falling.

The kind of Penny who ran into lakes without thinking about being pulled under by slimy, scaly creatures.

The kind of Penny who escaped from her crib as a baby, who knew what to say to make friends on the first day of school, who my mom called *bullheaded*. I remember that last one, because I went into the bathroom to check my head for horns in the mirror when she said it.

Before that Halloween night, I was a dauntless, bullheaded Penny.

Then Halloween happened.

A Halloween like changing the costume of Penny from the inside out.

The sun had been down for hours, and I basked in the light

from the streetlamps and in being allowed to stay up past my normal seven-year-old bedtime. I'd been out trick-or-treating with Mom and Dad all night (I was a ninja that year) and my painted pillowcase was stuffed full of chocolate and bold-colored candy and happy, sweet anticipation. It was finally time for bed.

My mom tucked me in under my big green quilt. She brushed the hair from my face, then turned off the light, and I stared at the silhouette of the fan spinning around and around and around. Spinning like my sugar-buzzed head.

Then I heard the rumbling sound.

The rumbling sound coming from under my bed.

The rumble was low and quiet. I could feel it rattling in my bones. The sound contained both hiss and growl, a tingle in my skin and an echo in my ear. The sound seemed to talk to me in my head, and whirled underneath me like waves pulled by an undertow.

But seven-year-old Penny was not afraid of monsters.

Seven-year-old Penny knew how to make friends.

In the faint streetlight coming through my window, I scooched out of bed, snuck quietly into the hall, and got my pillowcase of candy from the spot in the hallway closet where Mom had stashed it. Because to me, in that moment, the rumbling communication was clear and obvious.

The monster under my bed was hungry.

So I took a handful of candy from the bag. We left cookies for Santa, so why not Halloween candy for under-the-bed monsters?

I knelt with the candy, looking under my bed. I couldn't see much in the shadow and dim light, and when I stretched my hand into the dark, I didn't feel anything there, either, besides a lost sock. But not seeing any hungry monsters under my bed didn't deter me. I'd read and heard plenty of stories about monsters and other mythical creatures that could come and go and might not always be visible. In that center spot right under the bed, deep in the shadows and dust, I left a little pile of Snickers and Twix and Twizzlers. I wasn't stingy.

And then I got back in bed and slept deep deep deep.

The candy was gone when I woke up.

Something else was there instead.

Under my bed, in the same spot where I'd left the pile of candy, was a caramel apple, carefully wrapped in gold foil.

It all seemed so obvious to me, at the time. A natural gift exchange. And I knew I couldn't tell my mom, because that would only get the apple confiscated. *No sugar for breakfast,* she'd say. I didn't want to hurt my monster's feelings.

So I unwrapped the monster's treat from its foil. I took a large bite, crunching through the thick caramel as best I could. I even remembered to tell my monster thank you.

The sugary glaze was too sweet. The apple was soft, mealy, with brown spots. Sour juice dripped down my chin. But I didn't want to offend my monster, so I ate the treat he'd left for me.

I accidentally swallowed one of the small oval seeds.

The monster's treat didn't make me sick to my stomach. Not quite. Instead, it was as if the apple went to my head. Suddenly, and all through the morning, my thoughts kept getting twisted and turned and thrown upside down, like my brain was on a roller coaster. It even felt, sometimes, like my lungs were also along for the ride and I couldn't quite inhale properly. Everything looked just a tiny bit different, the way grass and trees and people's faces look different after a big gray cloud pushes its way in front of the sun. Only this time the cloud was inside me.

All day I kept blinking, my eyes kept drying out, and I realized I was staring. Not at anything in particular, but like something in me, something raw, was staring at the sky and knew a storm was coming.

I remember my mom asked me what I wanted for dinner that night, and I couldn't remember what I liked to eat. I couldn't remember anything good I'd ever tasted.

After that, I became a very different kind of Penny.

A Penny who'd let the Fear Maker in.

I learned his name in my nightmares.

That's when they started, the nightmares. Not like any nightmares I'd had before. These ones always had a tall man, the Fear Maker. These nightmares showed me blank eyes and the house in the woods the Fear Maker had started building. These, I felt in my marrow. These, I've felt ever since.

The story changes, but the end is always the Fear Maker. In the nightmares I am playing outside, Dad pushing me on the swings. Or I'm driving with Mom, listening to our favorite Broadway song. We sing and laugh. At first.

And then the Fear Maker finds me. He always finds me. Like a sudden storm, like a swarm of locusts, the Fear Maker descends. At first I can't see him, but I know he's there, a body of nightmare and shadow.

Then I do see him, right next to me, eyes glowing as red as embers, skin sallow. And his grin is so wide, his laugh is so loud, as he reaches down Mom's or Dad's throat, pulling their soul, their them-ness, out through their mouth. Then like an inescapable tide he washes away, taking the soul with him, his laugh echoing as he recedes.

And then the nightmare just gets worse.

Because when Mom or Dad looks at me, it's not them. Not really. It's just their shell, staring at me through blank, color-less, empty eyes.

I try to scream. Try to run for help. But wherever I go, who-ever I run to, they turn around and look at me with those same blank eyes.

That's when I wake up, and hear his laughter still ringing in my ears.

That's when I would run to Grandma's room, and she would read me poems and tuck me in between the words.

Except today I saw the blank, soul-devoured eyes in real life.

This time the emptiness came out of my nightmares into the real world.

Like the Fear Maker has been waiting ever since I swallowed that seed four Halloweens ago. Waiting and growing growing growing, like every day that I grow, he does too. Growing like the seed I sometimes still feel wriggling inside me. Growing until he's powerful enough to reach out of dreams and into real life.

I don't know how to wake up from that.

The Dark

The problem
with the dark
is that you can't see
what's waiting for you.

What's coming for you—
an unseen grip
on your ankle,
your throat.

Does the sun know
how much dark there is to
reach across
to turn on the light?

The dark,
an unknown
shape
in your bed.

Did you lock the door?
Did you check for eyes—
for someone
looking back at you?

What's the Answer?

Penny, I asked you a question.

Mr. Reitman stands at the front of the classroom, arms folded. Thick white hair, thick square glasses, thick bushy unibrow, grumpy and salty across his forehead. Glaring at me.

I don't know the answer. I don't understand how to multiply three numbers by three numbers. That many numbers is too many.

I don't know. I whisper the words, my head down, staring at my desk, at the fresh pencil scrapes along the front edge. I don't mean to scratch it up. I know it's a bad habit. A habit that happens when I feel the ice water shot at the top of my spine that freezes up my stomach, then shoots through the rest of my body, all the way to my ears and fingertips. When life and school and people are just too much and my guts do roller-coaster loops. When I feel the Fear Maker laughing at me.

There are a lot of pencil marks.

I'm looking down, so I don't see if Mr. Reitman sneers or rolls his eyes before he moves on to someone else. But I imagine it.

There are a lot of faces in this classroom. Moving from elementary to middle school this year means there are some familiar faces, but many new ones, too. The twins I sat next to

last year, ate lunch with, went to recess with, they moved to San Antonio over the summer. I see the boy who let his pet rat loose during show-and-tell in fourth grade. There's Gracie and Eun-tak, who braid each other's hair and have for years. But the crowd is also full of new faces, from other elementary schools. I don't know these faces well yet, because I'm still too scared to look up. It took a long time for me to feel comfortable chatting with the twins.

Mom says: *Patience.*

Mom says: *Be kind and give it time.*

Mom says: *It's only the third week of school, don't worry.*

But that many faces is too many.

Someone else gives the right answer to the math problem, breezy like it's nothing, like it's background noise, like bees humming or wind rustling the browning September leaves. I hope Mom is right. The ice on the back of my neck tells me she isn't.

I try to keep focused on the world of the classroom. The wooden desks. The pencils and erasers and the picture of an old man named Pythagoras up above the whiteboard. But my thoughts keep being pulled outside, into the Fear Maker's world, like the trees themselves are peering in at me, beckoning. I think of the thick woods behind our house and the close, towering pines outside my bedroom window. I know that's where he is. Where he lives, now that he's got a foothold here in our waking world. Where he's building his house.

I saw it once. Saw it in the daytime, when I was awake.

Years ago, when I'd finally decided to see if what my night-mares were showing me was really there.

It was there for real. And seeing it only made the night-mares worse.

Sitting here at my desk, I flinch just thinking about it.

And it's grown since then, the Fear Maker's house. I've watched it in my nightmares, growing all the time. New rooms, new walls, new creaking floors. If my nightmares are correct, since I saw it with my waking eyes, the house has grown an even bigger, more rickety porch, holding an empty rocking chair. It's grown closed shutters, which make the house seem as if at any moment, it will open its window eyes and wake up. There's a huge, leafless tree out front, beyond the porch, with branches and twigs that look like finger bones. In my nightmares I've seen a tall, locked door in an eerie room in the middle of that house, a door I've spent many nightmares trying to open, never succeeding. After that first time, I don't want to go see if my nightmares are right.

But here, now, I'm in a classroom. A classroom in Idaho, and I need to focus on numbers and faces and the paper in front of me.

My notebook in front of me.

Something to ease the cold in my spine and gut, the shriv-eling of my lungs like grapes shriveling into raisins. How to convince my insides that I am just a girl in a classroom, and that my shallow breaths are not the Fear Maker tracking me, that the woods themselves are not following me, getting closer.

I open my notebook. I jot a few lines.

Grandma, you told me to write my nightmares and fears. You told me to put them in poems.

Is there enough ink to write them all?

The Fear Maker

Blank eyes, full-throated fear, nightmares all
come from the same place.
The Fear Maker.

He lives in the deepest woods, under
the shadowiest trees, the ones
with eyes and bones.

Once upon a time, I saw the underside
of sleep and the Fear Maker
woke up.

He lives in a hungry, hungry house.
He moves in the shadows of snakes.
He drops into your tangled hair.

He watches me. He devours.

He smells like burnt rubber.
A litter box.
An open freezer.

He sounds like an old, old rocking chair.
A knocking at midnight.
Scissors cutting hair right behind your ear.

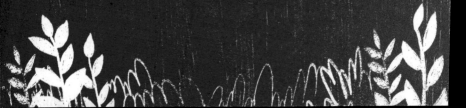

The world is his ocean and he waits like a shark.
Waits to swallow souls until there's nothing left
but blank, empty eyes.

Once upon a time, I offered a treat,
and the Fear Maker
tricked, looked in my direction

and started
slowly
walking.

Come Here, Penny

I'm running. My parents are gone and I'm in a big city, a place with alleys and dimly lit streets lined with skyscrapers and all the streetlamps flickering. I stepped into the Fear Maker's house and now suddenly I'm here, in this bleak, perilous city.

I run and run.

There's always someone watching me, someone with white, blank eyes.

Come here, Penny, a voice says.

In the middle of the road a blank-eyed man beckons. *Come here, Penny.*

A woman in the doorway of a shop with a blinking neon sign. *Come here, Penny.*

I cover my ears to block the sound, but it's as if the voices ring in my head. The voices of those who've lost their souls to the Fear Maker.

They walk slowly, so slowly, always toward me, closing in, yet no matter how hard I run I can't get ahead of them.

I turn and run down a side street. Too late I realize it's a bricked-in alleyway.

A dead end.

My chest heaves, my throat's dry. I turn around. I'm backed up against the far wall. I hear the chorus of *Come*

here, Penny, come here, louder and louder, until suddenly . . . silence.

At the mouth of the alley, a shadow grows. A figure, thin, too tall, about to turn the corner into the alleyway and find me.

I hear laughing.

I wake up.

The Best Flowers in Coeur d'Alene

Morning. I lie there as a crack of sunlight seeps through a broken blind and traipses along my toes. I pick up the notebook Grandma gave me from my nightstand, from its regular spot next to her poetry book. I jot a few lines, try writing down the nightmare in a poem, like she said, but it's hard to get the words right.

Breathe in. Breathe out. Try to exhale the nightmare, like I've practiced with Mom and Dad. I look at the jar of pennies on my dresser that Mom and Dad have helped me fill over the years. I'm glad they want to help and are willing to try anything at all to make the icy clenching grip in my stomach go away, but it's working even less than usual. My skin prickles like the blank eyes are still watching me. I feel trapped. As if seeing those empty eyes in real life isn't bad enough, the nightmares seem to be getting worse.

I make it to the bathroom. The eyes in the mirror still, at least for this morning, my own. Brush my teeth. Brush my wispy brown hair. Put on jeans and a pale yellow T-shirt.

I open the door and smell bacon.

I hear voices coming from downstairs.

Low, tense, crackling like stormy branches. I only catch pieces as I grab my notebook and sneak past Grandma's old room and down the staircase. I hear the words *can't afford.*

The words *not making enough*. The words *while she's at school*. I've heard words like that more and more lately.

When I step into the kitchen, Mom and Dad look at me and quickly smile, like they're trying to erase marks on a whiteboard. But I still see the creases on their foreheads, the deep shadows under their eyes. (Not blank eyes, though.)

Morning, Penny pen pen, Dad says. *Bacon?* He's pretty good at smiling and talking like nothing's wrong, but I see the heavy worry on his face.

Hi, my girl, Mom says. Her shoulders fight a sigh. *How'd you sleep?*

My nightmare, the beckoning blank-eyed people—telling them about it—would only draw deeper lines on their already worried faces. The Fear Maker got power in the waking world because of me, and I'm the one who needs to figure out how to stop his growing reach. And what if it's this endless ocean of fear inside my mind that's feeding his power? Growing that Fear Maker seed in my belly? Like I'm the electricity slowly but surely charging him up, and he's nearing 100 percent. If anything, I need to figure out how to take some of Mom and Dad's anxiety, some of all our anxiety, and make it smaller, because maybe that will make the Fear Maker smaller, too.

Good, I say.

Dad scoops me a plate of bacon and eggs and I sit at the table with my parents and my breakfast and my notebook. (They're used to seeing me scribbling away at an open page, even during breakfast.) It's always best when Dad cooks.

Somehow Mom manages to burn anything she tries to make. Except for orange rolls. Her orange rolls are magic. I think the stress etched into Mom's and Dad's faces is probably why we haven't made orange rolls in a while.

Dad's pink cheeks and soft middle are reassuring for me this morning, and I'm glad to have them nearby. Same with Mom's pointy glasses and her hair in a loose popped-spring bun that make her look like she could conquer the world with a wink and the click of a pen. She volunteers at the library a lot when I'm at school. Does that have to do with what they were whispering about?

Can we make orange rolls sometime? I say. *And go buy the pillowcase paint for Halloween?*

Hmm? Mom says. *Oh yeah, that's a great idea.*

The worry-creases are still there. I've always known we didn't have a ton of money, but we had each other and Dad's flowers and that always seemed like enough. But maybe it's not anymore. Lately, and especially since Grandma's heart got really sick, both Mom and Dad walk like they have cement in their shoes and a continent on their shoulders.

I didn't use to worry so much about these kinds of things before that night the Fear Maker came. What if Grandma has another *minor cardiac event* and we can't do anything about it? (That's what the doctors called it, and it's the reason Grandma had to move out of her room down the hall and into Olympus Assisted Living, but there's nothing *minor* about it, if you ask me.) What if there are more and more sick hearts? More and more blank eyes? What if what if what if?

No, I can't think like that. At least I have to try not to, even though sometimes it seems like the what-ifs bust into my brain no matter what I do. Mom and Dad and Grandma have done a million and one things to help me since the nightmares began, even besides the midnight poems. Those breathing exercises, and cups of warm milk at three a.m. The jar of pennies on my dresser was their idea for collecting good luck with my name on it. Thick quilts and bright paintings to look over me at night. A new rose-shaped nightlight and lullabies. How can I tell them none of it's working? And not only that, the nightmares are getting worse?

What's your favorite flower today? I ask Dad. I can't count the number of times I've asked him that question. It's our question, our *How are you right now?*

He grins. *Well, I'm liking the yellow, so I think today I might say tiger eye pansies. They're a perfect blend of dazzling and quirky, just like you. What's yours today?*

Probably ... um, maybe an ocotillo, I say.

Whoa, Dad says, grinning. *That's a good one. So vibrant and hardy.*

I google tiger eye pansies on my phone. Dad's right. They're so bright and graphic, exactly the kind of vibe I could use after seeing those blank eyes in real life.

Graphic. Yellow. Bright. No more blank eyes. No more no more no more.

I really should get that painting for the shop, Dad says again, looking at my Van Gogh sunflower notebook and also sort of staring into space.

The best flowers in all of Coeur d'Alene are in Dad's shop. I imagine the Van Gogh painting hanging there, yellow flowers popping out of their vase like a hello to all the customers.

Dad picks at his eggs, still staring. Does he see branches, stems, petals? Or does he only see the thing, whatever it is, that we can't afford?

Haiku

Fear Maker weeds look
like flowers till you get close
and smell only rot.

Visitor

Today is a Penny-and-Grandma day, and I could use it.

I make it through school without seeing any more blank eyes, and afterward Mom drops me off at the front entrance of Grandma's retirement home. (Without cupcakes this time— not after the incident with the baker. Mom looked at me funny when I said *No cupcakes, please no cupcakes*, but she said *Okay*). Mom says: *Talk with Grandma, work on homework, maybe*, while she runs errands (errands mean Penny-and-Grandma time).

She waits and watches from the car while I walk past the tall, fancy columns and through the glass entry doors and into the lobby, where the woman at the front desk recognizes me, waves, and smiles from behind her bright red glasses. (I check her eyes: a normal, rich green.)

The lobby has a rock fountain in the center, with ornate chairs and couches all around, and piano music playing. Backpack slung over my shoulder, I walk down the hall past the dining room with the dark wood tables and the clinking crystal chandelier.

I've done this walk through the halls lots of times now, and can see Grandma's room in my head. When she first moved, her room felt so different from how it was back at our house, but I've gotten used to how it looks, and how Grandma's arms will open up when she sees me. I can picture where she's got her small white bed, her nightstand, her lamp, and of course, her bookshelf.

When Grandma moved in a few months ago, Dad brought over her small bookshelf and now all her poems are back in their right order—one thing, at least, as it was when she lived with us. As it should be.

Like I said, she used to live with us, in that room down the hall from mine. That was *really* as it should be. She'd been in that bedroom down the hall from me since before I can even remember. But sometimes hearts get too sick for regular people like me and Mom and Dad to take care of. Sometimes I hate that Grandma and her heart need more help than I can give.

The first time we visited Grandma here at her new place, I put a fresh copy of her book *Undergrowth* on top of her nightstand. Her old copy, the first one the publisher sent her fifteen years ago, the one with the creased spine and cover page signed by Grandma herself, is on my nightstand at home. Grandma signed that copy specially for me.

I don't understand a lot of the poems, but I like how the words taste on my tongue when I whisper them out loud to myself. One of my favorites is a poem called "Fear, or Not Growing Gardens." Those words, I have memorized.

This time, on this visit, I have my sunflower notebook clutched tight against my chest, filled with my own words and poems. I haven't shown anyone any of my poems for a long, long time, because what if I find out they're terrible?

I've brought the notebook with me to Grandma's place

before (I bring it everywhere, of course) but this time feels a little bit different, because as I walk to Grandma's door, I think that maybe—a small, little maybe—I could show her one of my poems. If I'm not too afraid.

But her door is open and she's not alone.

There's a boy in Grandma's room. The boy is looking at the books on Grandma's shelf, and Grandma's sitting in her cozy chair by the window, smiling at him.

After a few seconds, Grandma sees me frozen in the doorway.

It's my lucky Penny, she says. *Come in, come in.*

I step through the door. The boy turns and looks at me. Both his and Grandma's eyes are normal, but a stranger in the room still makes me nervous.

The boy is wearing a button-down shirt and tie. He has a round face, soft arms, and a soft middle like my dad. His thick dark hair is parted neatly on one side and he smiles at me big. A whole-face smile. I try to smile back, but I don't know who he is or why he's there, and he's throwing off the picture in my head of what I expected to see when I came to Grandma's room.

This is Aarush Banerjee, Grandma says. *His mom works here, and sometimes Aarush comes and does his homeschool lessons. He's in sixth grade, too, aren't you, Aarush?*

He steps forward quickly, too fast, and nearly trips, catches himself, reaches out a hand. *Hi!*

I take his hand even though I'm nervous. It's warm, and his eyes are bright like he's excited to meet me. But now I'm definitely not going to read my poetry, not with a random boy in the room.

Hi, I say.

Then I'm not sure what to do with my hand. I'm afraid of the swelling moment of quiet, the gurgling in my stomach. When I start remembering how I don't know what to say, never know what to say, I hear the Fear Maker's voice in my mind confirm all the worst thoughts I have about myself, like he's trying to make those thoughts harden in me like cement. His voice is always even, crisp, and smooth, like the skin of a bright apple.

Yes, says his voice in my head, *you somehow manage to be both incredibly weird and extremely dull. Who'd want to befriend a boring, strange little thing like you?*

But those thoughts can't go on for too long, because Aarush speaks—in a rush and all at once.

Your grandma is awesome, he says, and his words are louder than the voice in my head. *She read me some poems. I don't understand them all, but I like how they sound. My mom works in the office. Doing their accounting stuff. I'm going to be a doctor someday. Are you here on Tuesday and Thursday afternoons? I am. Maybe we can work on homework together? What's your favorite movie? I like* Babe, *with the farmer and the talking pig. I like your notebook. Are you a poet, too?*

He talks and it's like being on a merry-go-round spinning faster and faster and I'm nervous about falling off, but his speeding, breathless enthusiasm, like the wind, makes me grin in spite of myself. For a second I'm sort of sad about Grandma sharing our thing with this new boy, but he's so excited about it and about how cool Grandma is (he's right), and his bubbling, happy voice is helping distract me from the Fear Maker's voice in my head, so I can't be upset for too long. I'm not sure what to say, but his excited puppy-dog chatter makes me a tiny bit less nervous about that than I was before. I hold my notebook closer. *Um.*

It's okay, Aarush says, like he can tell what I'm thinking. *You don't have to read your stuff to me or anything. We could do math homework, or watch a movie with your grandma or something. Wanna do that?*

Grandma's bed is angled into the corner on the far side of the room, and the table, the bookshelf, and Grandma's big comfy chair are in the other far corner, by the big window. I look toward the table.

Um, yeah, maybe some homework would be good, I say. *I'm Penny, by the way.*

Aarush grins, opening his backpack and taking out his math book. *Great to meet you, Penny!* he says.

I bring my backpack over, put my notebook on the table, and take the chair opposite him, facing away from the door. Grandma watches me for a second, smiling, before opening the book she has on her lap.

Do you like math? Aarush says. *It's probably my best subject. Math and drawing.*

Um, I say. *Not really. I'm not very good at it,* I admit.

Here, show me what you're working on, Aarush says, sliding around the table and looking at the math worksheet I've just pulled out of its folder. My face and hands get warm at first, having a stranger so close to me, but he just looks at my paper and seems so natural and unembarrassed that even I start feeling less awkward about it, and pretty soon he's showing me a trick for calculating circumference that somehow makes it click more than it ever has before. Back in fifth grade, it took me weeks and weeks to get comfortable being friends with the twins and chatting with them during lunch, before they moved, but somehow Aarush makes it extra easy.

After a few minutes of working on math, Aarush goes back to the other side of the table and pulls out a book. *Numbers and shapes make sense,* he says. *It's essays that are hard, and analyzing books, you know? Especially when the whole book is told in poems. My teacher says there is counting and rhythm in a lot of poetry, but I'm not sure I get it yet.*

Grandma sits up tall in her chair. *A book in poems? Which one?*

Aarush shows us the book he's reading for homeschool— *The Red Pencil* by Andrea Davis Pinkney.

Verse novels go all the way back to the ancient Greeks, Grandma says. *Don't read it at first with your analytical brain. Read it with your experience brain. How do the poems make you feel? What's the experience of the story in your own mind? The analysis will come later.*

We're both looking at Grandma, listening close. She laughs at herself. *Ha, I was an English professor, in case you can't tell,* she says to Aarush. *I guess I still can't turn it off.*

Aarush bops a little in his seat. *I love it!* he says. *That's the most helpful thing anyone's said about how to read this book.*

Aarush stops for a moment, staring at the book, then back at Grandma. *I wonder . . .* He pauses, and I can almost see the fireworks popping in his mind. *I wonder if that could be the same for science, too? I mean, like . . . could you, I dunno, look for the cure for cancer with a sort of poetry experience kind of brain and then go to the analysis?*

Brilliant, Grandma says.

I click my pen, trying to put together what Aarush said in my own mind. Looking at science like it's a poem? What would that even mean? If someone could find a cure for cancer that way, could they also find a cure for blank eyes and empty souls?

Maybe this is a step toward figuring out how to banish the Fear Maker and heal what he's hurt. Can a poem take the seed of something traumatic and grow something good?

I watered the desert from my aorta until a scab became a tree. I whisper the words from "Fear, or Not Growing Gardens," a habit I barely notice.

And the seed in the fruit in the husk was me and the camel that swallowed was me, Aarush says, continuing the line. *That's one of my favorites.*

Grandma's soft, crepe-paper cheeks are beaming. *And the garden he fertilized was boundless and also me.* She finishes the line. *Oh, you two, you make an old poet's heart happy.*

I talk with Grandma and Aarush, feeling less buzzing and anxious than I have in a while. For just a minute, my math worksheet doesn't seem like it's going to wrap itself around my head and smother me. For just a minute, Grandma's voice feels like

I'm home again. Home and safe. For just a minute, I'm actually with a person my age and not wishing I had a shell to protect me, not looking for ways to escape. Words still come from my mouth in the normal small drip-drips, like a mostly turned-off faucet, not full blast like they do for Aarush, but at least I don't feel like running away.

Then there's a knock on Grandma's door. The squeaking sound of opening hinges.

Sorry to interrupt the party, a voice says. *Medicine time.*

Grandma looks toward the door. Smiles. *Oh, hi, Gladys. Gladys, this is my granddaughter, Penny, and our friend Aarush.*

I turn around and it's a woman in pink scrubs, a blond ponytail, a name tag on a lanyard. A woman with a tray of tiny plastic cups full of pills in her hands.

A woman with white teeth and blank, hollow, nothing-in-them eyes.

Medicine

My throat bobs and I swallow back a scream. My hands white-knuckle the chair I'm sitting in, but all I want is to run away run away run away. One hand slides to my notebook, gripping tight—I really could bolt any second.

If only the floor would open up, the wooden boards peel back, and me and this chair could fall through, to somewhere—anywhere—else.

The woman in pink steps into the room, bringing the little cup of pills to Grandma. I flinch with each step, but Grandma reaches out and takes the medicine as if everything is completely normal. The woman in pink looks at me and smiles.

A blank-eyed smile that just looks like hunger.

Like she's a great white shark and I'm the chum.

Grandma swallows the medicine like it's nothing, like she doesn't see that the woman bringing it to her has colorless, staring, white-marble eyes. Aarush says hello like he doesn't see anything abnormal, either. He says, *We're working on math homework.* He says, *Have you read Grandma Penelope's poems?*

They don't see it. Neither of them. I stay silent, as usual. Maybe it really is me who's losing it, whose brain is dropping blank-eyed images like withered petals—one by one.

Suddenly, it feels like the shadows from the forest, from my dreams, are getting closer and closer, because with this woman in the room, all I can think about is my nightmares.

With her looking at me with those nothing-eyes, smiling, I only see the Fear Maker, and he makes me think of every car crash and earthquake I've ever seen on TV, every minor cardiac event that became a major life change, everything scary that could possibly happen. If his real-world control keeps growing, will it get strong enough to make awful, horrible things like that happen? It feels like all the faces at school are turning and staring at me. I'm alone in the thickest part of the forest, where the sun never, ever comes up.

My heart is a creature caught in a trap looking for a way out. I've got to do something. Anything.

I break my fingers' stiff grip on the chair and rub my eyes. My brain churns like a tornado, searching for something solid, something bright to pull into itself. Anything. What's my dad's favorite flower again? What's that song Mom is always humming off-key? I can't can't can't remember the words to anything.

I stare hard at the woman for as long as my jittering nerves will allow. Her eyes do not change.

Thank you, Gladys, Grandma says.

Before Gladys leaves, she looks at me with those empty eyes and her smile widens. She winks.

The shadows in the room grow and grow.

The Fear Maker's House

My nightmares are welcome mats
to the Fear Maker's house.
His greedy, greedy house
that I walked to, once,
to test nightmares in the real world.
The house—very real—grows
in the woods and my dreams.

The Fear Maker and his house—
a devouring mollusk in a shell.

I've seen the house
with open eyes, and closed, too.
I feel the house's open mouth
behind me, always hungry.
For bones, blood, feathers,
for each of my heartbeats,
one, two, three.

This house has a stomach
that can never be filled. A stomach
behind a tall, locked door
at the center of this labyrinth
where the Fear Maker keeps

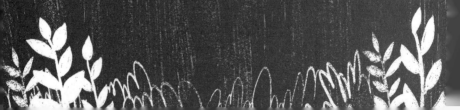

all his trapped souls,
leaving nothing but blank eyes.

Deep in the woods, the Fear Maker lives
in his greedy, greedy house,
an expanding, growing house
with plenty of rooms to spare.

That day I found it
with my waking eyes, I immediately
knew that if I went
inside
I would never step out again.

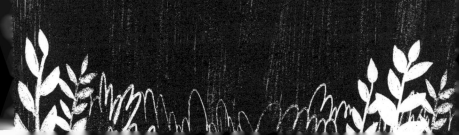

Are You Okay?

What's wrong, lucky Penny? Grandma asks. I realize there are lines on my palm where I've been gripping the spiral side of my notebook.

Did you . . . did you notice her eyes? I whisper. *Did you see?*

Grandma frowns, concerned. *Her eyes? I didn't notice anything in particular. Although Gladys has been acting a tiny bit unlike herself lately. A touch more melancholy than I remember from when I moved in.*

I look at Aarush.

He shrugs. *I thought they were normal brown?*

So it's just me. Even Grandma can't see them.

Never mind, I say.

There's a muddy bird's nest in my throat and it's hard to swallow.

Should I say something? Do I need to warn Grandma, and how do I do that without sounding absolutely bonkers? Or what if, because I'm the only one who sees the blank eyes, I'm supposed to help? Could I help Gladys? But even if I tried to help, or confronted one of the blank-eyed people directly, would that do any good at all? Or would it be like cutting a weed but leaving the root?

You okay, sweetheart? Grandma says.

Fine.

We'll see you next week, says Aarush.

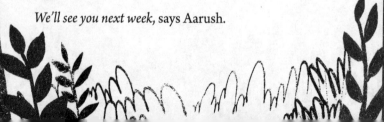

Fine.

How was Grandma's? asks Mom as we drive home.

Fine.

Are you okay? she adds. *You seem even quieter than normal.*

Am I okay? I'm trying not to think about eyes, about shadows. About whether Grandma is okay there, whether her heart is okay in there. About how little there actually is between Mom's and my feet and the gravelly, deadly asphalt we're speeding over at sixty-five miles an hour. About nightmares in the woods coming to life and what I can possibly do to stop them before they crash into me and break my world to pieces.

How nobody can see them but me.

Fine.

Fine.

Fine.

Crash Poem

Car
    Crash
Felled tree
    Crash
Earthquake
    Crash
Can't afford
    Crash
One wrong move
    Crash
Wrong answer
    Crash
Bones
    Crash
Bad heart
    Crash
Something always
    Just above you
Waiting
    Waiting to
        Crash

Nothing

I wake up sweating again.

Another nightmare. This time it was my dad. I followed him into the Fear Maker's house, but then suddenly we were in a rocky, stormy place, gray clouds twisting above us, and Dad was running up a hill, and in my dream I knew the steep ridge on the other side of the hill meant death. I couldn't scream for him. I couldn't catch up to him fast enough. He tumbled tumbled tumbled over the ridge, just before I reached out to save him. But when I looked over the ledge, my dad was gone. It was someone else standing there at the bottom of the cliff, staring up at me, grinning.

The story may change, but the end is always the Fear Maker.

My throat clutches and my hands are shaking. My head still rings with the echoes of his laughter. Despite how many times I've been through this, I'm not used to it. Can't get used to it.

I go out into the hall toward the bathroom. Stepping softly, I try not to wake my parents, because they're exhausted, too, and because I don't want them to ask me why I'm awake. Instead, I sip some water and splash a handful under my shadowed, wide eyes.

Back to my room. Breathe in and out, in and out. I'll try again to write this down, like Grandma said. It's just a nightmare, I tell myself, like I've practiced with Mom and Dad so many times before. But it's *not* just a nightmare, not from what I've seen, and no matter how many times I repeat it in my head I can't make myself believe it. So what mantras and strategies am I supposed to use now?

I walk toward my bed, about to step up and slide under the covers.

A cold, clammy hand grips my ankle tight.

My whole body freezes, too petrified to scream.

Every muscle in my body feels pumped through with shock and terror, like I've just been shot out of a cannon and into space.

The hand around my ankle clenches harder.

Whimpering, I look down.

As I do, the grip vanishes, and there's nothing there.

I force myself to reach over to my nightstand and turn on my lamp. I take large steps back back back, away from the bed. It seems an age that I stand there, paralyzed, until I'm ready to bend my legs and look under the bed. Inside me I can somehow feel that caramel apple seed I accidentally swallowed growing bigger, heavier, sprouting sharp little tendrils. As I check the under-bed shadows, I just hope that, if I need to, I'll be able to scream.

Slowly, shaking, I crouch down and peer beneath my bed.

There's nothing there.

Nothing at all.

I shine my phone flashlight into each corner. Nothing.

But something was there.

I can still feel the ghost of the Fear Maker's grip.

First the real-life, soul-sucked, blank-eyed people, and now this? Until I saw the baker's eyes, I thought the Fear Maker could reach me only in my dreams. He's put trembling in my thoughts and in my heart, but this is the real, actual world. This is the Fear Maker I let loose, eating the souls of the people around me. As if my fear is feeding and feeding that Fear Maker seed in my gut. More evidence that his hold on me—on this world—is getting stronger and stronger.

Somewhere Nowhere Someone Anyone

Pale gray light peers in through the blinds as I stand there by my bed. My T-shirt is soaked through with sweat from a night of monsters real and dreamed, and my foggy head hasn't quite recovered. I look around my room, trying to orient myself through my stiff shoulders, through the welling nightmare in my eyes. This is my room, isn't it? Pastel blue walls. Mason jar on my dresser filled with pennies from the year I was born.

It's not working: deep breaths, looking at all that's familiar—it's not grounding me, not calming me down, and I can't think of anything that will.

I want to talk to my parents about my nightmares and the Fear Maker's growing power, unburden myself of a little bit of this. But if even after seeing the white eyes and feeling the bony grip myself, I still barely believe everything that's going on, then how can I possibly hope anyone else will believe me? And at the same time, I want to think without talking to anyone, want space to really figure out what's happening. I want time alone and also not to be alone. I want somewhere to sit and be, but not here, not anywhere I know. I pace across the carpet, trying not to wake my parents.

Minutes tick tick tick by. I don't want to sleep or sit or walk.

Finally, I decide I may as well shower and rinse some of the sweat and night terror and monster grip off my skin. I quick quick quick head to the bathroom.

My face in the mirror looks like someone else's. Pasty gray skin, sweat-plastered hair, gaunt cheeks. I can't help but imagine myself looking back with my soul gone, with those blank eyes, and fear rushes over me like a tidal wave, a tsunami.

Too much. Too much.

What what what what what

Do

I

Do?

Then I notice the light.

Yellow light, warm, shining faintly from behind the glass shower door.

Natural light no bulb could make.

There's sunlight here, in my bathroom.

The hairs on my arms stand up, and I feel my heartbeat, thrum thrum, alive and expectant, like my skin cells are aching for that light. Like this is the truest form of daylight, to blast away every trace of nightmare. Am I imagining it, or really feeling that soothing glow on my arms and hands and face? Either way, the relief it brings is pure and swift. My hands like monarch butterflies warming their wings after frost, I reach for the shower door.

Pull it open.

My eyes squint, flooded with bright light.

I step through.

Garden, My Garden

The world—the light—resolves itself into sunflowers sunflowers sunflowers as far as I can see. Sunflowers I could swim through clear to the horizon.

I gasp, dazed, my lungs breathing more than oxygen. I inhale bright blue open sky, exactly what my capillaries have needed all this time.

If the Fear Maker's world is night, this one is morning. Every part of me seems to sense right away that none of the Fear Maker's fingers, none of his powers, nothing from his realm can reach me here. Here, the Fear Maker would be like a speck of ash disintegrating in the wind.

I take one step, then another, and I know I could walk forever. Never once get tired or hungry. The muscles above my shoulder blades feel as though I've been carrying a backpack of bricks, and here, now, I can finally set it down.

I can't get enough of this breathing.

Gently, I touch a sunflower's yellow petals, splayed around its deep brown center. They seem to greet me back, little gentlemanly petal princes kissing my fingertips.

Grandma's poem, my favorite one, keeps going through my mind. The line *One filament, one petal, each more than fear can make.* She would love it here. She could make so many poems about this place. I think of the flower painting on the cover of my notebook and imagine Van Gogh could do beautiful things with this place, too.

The path through the flowers turns according to my whim. Left, right, always room enough to walk through. The sunflowers are the perfect height for me to smell and see across, until I wonder what it would be like to let them cover me, so I could see the flowers from underneath. As soon as I think it, I turn onto a path where the flowers tower a foot, two feet above me, and I can see their fuzzy green undersides, radiating like mini lions' manes. I could cocoon myself in this flower blanket—this safety—forever, but I also feel the light pushing me forward, like I could run forever and never stop.

The soil under my feet is soft and rich and dark, and I'm glad not to be wearing shoes. I find a few scattered sunflower seeds on the ground and put them in my pajama pants pocket.

There's nobody else here, not that I can see, but I wonder about who made this place, who loved it into existence. I would like to talk to them, whoever they are.

Ahead is a bench, wrought-iron intricate swirls and swooshes along its back, painted a clean, bright mint green. Yes, I think, I would like to sit. Sit and be, for a moment, in this sunflower place.

I can see forever from where I sit, endless sunflower fields clear to the horizon. In this stillness I register a thought, a malicious voice I no doubt brought into this garden with me, trying to tell me I'm confused, seeing things. But that voice has never been more pathetic, more muted, and it barely registers before evaporating. And oh, just that evaporation makes me laugh. That voice, those thoughts—how utterly unimportant they are in the face of these flowers! How teensy and untrue!

For hours, minutes—both, neither—I sit in the sunflower garden. I wish I could bring Mom and Dad here. I wish I could bring Grandma, and even Aarush. They would be safe here. Safe from the Fear Maker and everything he does.

But when I think of them, I know it's time to go back. Not back home, because this place is more Home than anywhere I've ever been, but back to them, back to Mom and Dad, because they're Home, too.

I leave my green bench and walk awhile longer, until I see a little cottage. Brick, thatched roof, bright white shutters. Before, when I came into the garden, there was no cottage, no door—I just found myself surrounded by dazzling flowers. But to get back to my room, my world, I know that cottage door is where I need to go, and I take slow steps toward it, letting each of my toes feel the ground. I look at it for a while before I turn the unlocked knob of the wooden door. It creaks when I open it.

I step inside.

Going Back

I'm back in my bathroom. Back in the still, gray light of the shower. I check the clock on my bathroom wall and not a minute has passed since I left.

My skin feels squeaky clean, my hair fresh, like I did in fact just shower. But my shoulders are already beginning to ache, like I've picked up that load of bricks again. My body feels sore all over and my eyes can't blink away the exhaustion.

It's so early. I stumble back to bed and collapse on top of my green comforter, the one with faded buttons at the corners, the one I've had since I was five that used to be better at keeping away the nightmares. According to the little alarm clock on my nightstand, there's still an hour or so for sleep, which I suddenly need more than ever.

What just happened?

A sunflower garden in the shower?

Are you stupid, Penny?

I jump. Look around.

Nobody's there.

But I heard the voice. Heard it this time with my actual ears, not just the voice in my nightmares, the voice in my head echoing all the worst things going through my mind. A voice I could have sworn I heard right behind me. Aloud, I notice an edge to this flat, satin-smooth voice I hadn't picked up on before.

It sounds irritated.

I found the Garden and now the Fear Maker sounds angry. The volume is at full blast.

I curl up into myself, pressing my face into the cool pillow, that fear seed in my belly twirling and tendriling. *Go away go away go away*, I think. *No more nightmares. I'm so tired. Please.*

What if the voice is right?

Did I really just find a sunflower garden in my shower? What if I'm hallucinating? Maybe it's all a delusion. Maybe the blank-eyed people are just the nightmares finally cracking my brain like a rotten nut. I'm starting to feel as powerless as I did standing in front of the Fear Maker's house in the woods years ago, that same breathless clutching in my lungs like I'm being tossed around on a loop-the-loop and there's not enough air.

I can imagine trying to explain all this to someone, and what they might say. I lie there trying to decide if I should tell, who I should tell. Mom and Dad? Even if they listened, carefully, thoughtfully—even if they wanted to believe—I can already see the concerned look on Mom's face, her hand reaching out to check my forehead. Dad making a call and saying, *We're gonna take you to talk to someone who might be able to help.* I'm sure talking to a professional would help, probably in lots of ways, but they would be even less likely to believe me than Mom and Dad. And what about the money it would cost?

But that Garden. It was so, so real. It felt so right and safe, so much larger and more substantial than the waking world, or even the Fear Maker's world.

Now I'm back here, in this world, this house, this room. My room. Which is just . . . normal. Back to a world where everything is heavy and I am afraid of things.

Back to a world where the nothing-eyed people, the ones with their souls trapped by the Fear Maker, have stepped out of my nightmares.

I hear a grin in the voice. I didn't know that was possible, but that voice, the Fear Maker's voice from the thickest part of the woods, is laughing, watching me toss-turn, toss-turn. He doesn't need nightmares to see me now.

But that garden.

I turn over and feel a lump in my pocket. I reach my fingers into the shallow pocket of my pajama pants. There. Three large sunflower seeds.

Real.

Real seeds, and still here in my pocket.

I wrap my hand around them. The relief is a cool breeze. With the seeds clutched tight in my palm, I drift off into a deep, Pacific Ocean kind of sleep where at least this time, for once, there are no nightmares.

Yellow

I wish I could carry the color
yellow
in a jar
yellow
in my cupped hands
but
yellow is slippery
and when I move too fast
I'm afraid
it will slip through
my fingers.

Miscalculations

I sit at my desk, head down, and wait for class to start.

While I wait, I flip past pages of jotted lines and poems and open my notebook to a blank page. I have those sunflower seeds in my pocket, that Garden air still in my lungs, and I think I'm ready to plan and start a list of things I could try that might dispel the Fear Maker from the waking world. But so far, my idea list has exactly nothing.

It was all kinds of relief, waking up to find those seeds still in my pocket. Not vanished or imagined. Maybe I will try looking up today, up at all the faces. Maybe, miraculously, I'll know what to say to the girl who sits next to me in math who always wears mismatched socks that still seem to go together somehow. Today her socks are black and pink.

I hear a buzzing from the front pocket of my backpack. I unzip the front pocket, take out my phone, and keep it hidden under the desk. Just a quick check.

A text from an unknown number:

Hi Penny! Aarush here! Your grandmother gave me your number, I hope that's okay. My mom found this contest where you send in a poem and a picture and I know we're only in sixth grade but these kinds of things could look good on college applications and

I like to draw but I don't think I could write a good
poem and there can be two people and the winners
get $500 and would you want to do it with me?

I read the text a couple of times. It sounds just like Aarush,
that rush of words all at once. He wants me to enter a contest
with him? He's already thinking about college applications?
I remember him mentioning something about wanting to be
a doctor, I think. And how does he know my poems are any
good? What if they're terrible? And he wants me to send them
off, have strangers read them, have real people judge them?
My stomach flips and roils like I'm on a roller coaster and the
safety bar is loose.

Could I do that?

Could I let someone else see that deepest, bone-marrow-
level part of me?

A laugh fills the classroom. A big laugh, hard and steely.

Mr. Reitman.

He comes in and tosses his briefcase on the desk. I don't
think I've ever seen him toss anything before, let alone his
briefcase. Or heard him laugh.

Hey there, Penny, could you please put your phone away?
Thanks!

I realize my mouth is open and that I'm holding out my
phone for the world and the teacher to see. I nearly drop it
on the floor in my rush to stash it away. He could have gotten really mad. I could have gotten in serious trouble. That's

what I would have expected—phones are never supposed to be seen—and last week, Mr. Reitman sent a girl to the front office just for chewing gum.

Something's off.

I try to swallow down a lump of unease and lean toward Mismatched Socks Girl. There's that little whirlpool in my gut that kicks up every time I talk to someone new, someone I don't know very well, afraid I'm going to run out of words, or somehow use the wrong ones. Whether my poems are any good or not, writing words on a page is always so much easier. But I have to check one more time that it isn't just me, that this is real, so I lean in. *Do you . . . ?* I clear my throat. *Do you think he's acting kind of weird?*

She looks up at Mr. Reitman for a second, then shrugs. *Yeah, maybe a little,* she whispers. Then there's the hint of a smirk on her face. *Maybe having a good day just isn't like him.*

Isn't like him.

At least Mismatched Socks Girl can tell something's off. Like Grandma could with Gladys, even though she couldn't see the blank eyes. I feel the Fear Maker's apple seed sprouting deeper into my guts and bones, and maybe that has something to do with why I'm the only one who sees the full fruits of his nightmare labors. I feel helpless, like I'm watching a car crash. But even if I knew how to help Mr. Reitman this time, wouldn't the Fear Maker just come back again and again and again?

Is this how it starts? The soul-snatching? I imagine the shadow of the Fear Maker's hand reaching inside Mr. Reitman, playing him like a puppet up there in front of the class, before taking his soul back to that treacherous, crooked house in the woods, like in my dreams. That's what he does—takes away what's them, leaving what's not. I'd much rather have the real Mr. Reitman, cantankerous grump and all, than whatever this fakey-fake counterfeit is.

Mr. Reitman starts class with a discussion about right angles. Mr. Reitman, grinning wide wide wide.

At the end of class, as I walk out the door and pass his desk, I think I see something pale and cold shifting in his eyes.

Shoes

Walking up the driveway to the front door, Mom keeps looking at my feet.

There's a hole in your sneaker, she says.

I look down at the gray sidewalk and at my tennis shoes. There is, in fact, a small tear forming over the left pinkie toe. The ends of the laces are frayed and one is close to snapping. To be honest, I hadn't really noticed. To be honest, I've been too anxious about everything else. Do I need to be anxious about my shoes now, too?

Laces snapping, me tripping, face-planting, everyone watching in the middle of class?

I'll take you shoe shopping soon. I think I saw something about a clearance sale . . .

I think of the jar of pennies in my room. *We could use my pennies. I can save up even more.*

Oh, sweetie. That's so thoughtful, but no, no . . . I'll figure it out.

We don't have to buy paint for pillowcases this year, I say.

I look at my shoes. I would hate missing a year of painting pillowcases with Mom, but there are bigger things to worry about.

Mom sighs. Is she about to cry? *I think we have leftover paint from last year,* she says. We reach the front door and she slowly, distractedly digs through her purse for the key.

I try to think of something that will cheer her up.

I got a text from that boy I met at Grandma's. He seems nice.

That's great! I've been a little worried about you on the friend front since the twins left. Maybe you can help him with poetry while he helps you with math?

It's true Aarush does seem nice, but I still don't know about letting strangers see my poems, about trying to be friends with this random boy. What if he thinks I'm too weird?

Yeah, I manage to say. *Maybe.*

We should have him and his family over sometime, Mom says.

I keep quiet. She finds the key in her bag and unlocks the door. Before she opens it, she glances down at my feet again.

There's got to be . . . she says, softly trailing off. *We'll figure something out.*

She says it like she's holding up a wall and she's scared if she eases up for even a second, it will all collapse. Her mouth is trying to be firm, but I see worry. I see fear. She adjusts her glasses and grips the doorknob tight.

I close my eyes. It was so much easier in that Garden where all I needed was bare feet.

Pennies

A penny saved is
lost in the sewer grate.
A penny earned
doesn't buy laces
or worriless faces,
doesn't buy off the storm
clouds hanging low
threatening rain.
The pennies pile
Everest high, looming, steep,
and they keep coming, covering me deep
and they keep coming, covering me deep.

Rearranging

Before I go to bed again, I know something has to change.

My parents are downstairs watching TV while I stand in my doorway and stare into my room. I think of the cold, hard grip around my ankle. That must *not* happen again.

Maybe . . . maybe there's something about that spot. That spot on the floor, under the bed, where the hand grabbed me and the caramel apple appeared all those years ago.

And so I decide it's time for a little rearranging. I move my dresser from one wall to the other. I put the bookcase on the other side of the window, and it takes me a long time to pull all the books off and put them back on again. I drag my nightstand from one side of the room to the other, and my mom calls up when she hears the noise.

What's going on up there? she shouts over the hum of the TV newscaster. *Sounds like you're making a fort or something.*

Maybe if I were more grown-up, I would tell her that eleven-year-olds don't build forts. But I know the truth—that maybe I'm not grown-up at all, because I could use a fort really, really badly—and I call back, *Something like that.*

The volume on the TV gets lower, and soon there are steps coming up the stairs. Mom gives two quick knocks, then opens my door.

She stands and looks over my new layout.

I should have asked first, I say. *Sorry.*

Mom smiles. *It looks good*, she says. *I could have helped you, though. I didn't know you wanted to rearrange.*

I ... The urge came on kind of suddenly, I say. Close enough to the truth.

What do you have left? Can I help?

I think I'm okay. Just a few more books to put back.

Mom comes over and brushes a strand of hair from my face. *Okay. Tell me if you need anything, all right?*

I nod. It's a good thing to hear, even though I still don't know exactly how to tell her what I need. I'm not sure of it myself.

Mom pulls me in and kisses the top of my head. She smells like her favorite lavender lotion.

Thanks, Mom, I say.

She heads downstairs and I turn back to my room. I return the last few things to their spots in the closet, and the last few books to the shelves, and then finally there's an empty space where my bed used to be. Somehow I don't want to step into that corner, like if I do, I'll be sucked into the floor. But I can't just leave it empty like that. I need something to cover that spot.

I wish I could cover the spot with sunflowers.

For just a second, I close my eyes tight and try to feel that yellow light and warmth on my skin, that dark soil between my toes, but when I open my eyes again and check the nearby rooms, there's no glow coming from the shower door or my bedroom door or my closet door or anywhere.

Instead, I head out into the hall. There's a little table in the alcove between my door and the bathroom that used to have a clock on it until the clock broke. I take the table and bring it into my room and put it in the empty corner. Then I take my grandma's book of poems, that copy of *Undergrowth* that she signed for me, and lay it carefully on the table. I put my jar of pennies and my seeds from the Garden on the table, too.

The most protective things I have. The best barrier and fortress I can manage.

I guess we'll see what the Fear Maker makes of that.

Big Questions

The next time I walk through the lobby of Olympus Assisted Living, down the hall to Grandma's bedroom, I'm torn between wanting to walk slowly with my eyes wide open, checking for Gladys or anyone else who might now be one of the soul-trapped, blank-eyed people, and on the other hand, wanting to dash to Grandma's room quickly, hands up around my eyes like horse blinders, trying to see nothing around me at all. I walk slowly, in the end, but don't glimpse anything unusual. Maybe Gladys is off work today.

I wish again for some kind of magic soul-pill that could fix the emptiness. But I know that wouldn't stop the Fear Maker. Not really. He'd still come back and back and back. Besides, I know what I've seen. I don't think there's a way to fix the blank eyes without going back down that path through the trees, deep into the woods, walking up to the Fear Maker's front door, and knocking.

Nothing will be fixed until someone—me?—deals with the Fear Maker himself.

If I'm still, I can even sometimes feel that apple seed tugging lightly at my insides, like it's trying to get back to its maker in his hungry house.

But I'm just one eleven-year-old girl, and he's the Fear Maker. This would be like Little Red going face-to-face with the Big Bad Wolf, and she got devoured.

But this time, there's no kindly woodsman to set her free.

So far, it's only been strangers with empty eyes, but every day I feel the Fear Maker's reach getting closer. I feel that fear seed in me sprouting, like my dread and nightmares are its fertilizer, a vicious cycle of cancerous growth. The more the fear seed grows, the harder it is to stop it from taking root, and the Fear Maker's house gets bigger and bigger.

I keep imagining looking at someone I know, someone I love, and watching it happen to them. I imagine my mom lowering her book, face blanker than an empty page. I imagine asking my dad about his favorite flower, and him turning to answer, a wide grin on his face and nothing in his eyes.

I get closer to Grandma's door and have a thought that surprises me. I'm actually excited knowing that Aarush will probably be here today. I'm not ready to show him my poems yet, but he's easy to be with, and I don't feel the fear seed sprouting new tendrils when I try to talk to him. Typical Penny brain would be anxious about having to talk to someone sort of new, or frustrated at someone else being there during Penny-and-Grandma time. But not now. Not with Aarush.

When I reach her room, the door is open and he *is* there. I step inside, not as hesitant as last time.

Lucky Penny! says Grandma. She's in her chair again, and Aarush is at the table, his chair turned around to face Grandma while he shows her a page in a book. *Come, come, Aarush was just showing me something called the golden spiral.*

I learned about it for homeschool yesterday, he says. *It's kind of both math and art.*

I join Aarush at the table and he shows me pictures of nautilus shells and storm systems and flower petals, and then he shows me the math equation that connects them all together. It's beautiful and neat and tidy. I wish more things were so clear and ordered. I wish my brain and thoughts were golden spirals instead of what they actually feel like—scribbles, messy graffiti, and tangled yarn.

Grandma picks a book from her shelf and settles back into her comfy chair while Aarush and I do our homework at the table. His round cheeks have dimples that deepen when he's trying hard to focus. It doesn't feel awkward to work quietly together. I don't feel that gut-burble pressure to think of conversation, of the right, clever words, maybe because I know Aarush will have no problem chatting and starting up a conversation if he wants to. He talks so freely, and his open face doesn't look embarrassed or judgy about what I say, either.

After a while, he taps my hand and nods toward Grandma's chair. She's fallen asleep, the book of poems open on her knee. Aarush smiles, which makes me smile, too.

I wish I could sleep that easy, I whisper.

You don't sleep well? Aarush says, attempting a whisper.

Oh . . . I say, hesitating. I look at his open, warm eyes and the earnest worry line across his forehead. *I just . . . I get nightmares sometimes.*

Ah. Aarush nods. *My brother used to get night terrors. Those screaming episodes almost every night? Not fun. Next time I'll bring you some of the nighttime tea my mom makes for us when we can't sleep.*

I doubt a cup of tea will be effective against the Fear Maker, but at this point I'll try anything. And just having Aarush here wanting to help makes me feel less alone.

Thanks, I say.

It feels so good talking to someone that I'm brave enough to ask a very un-Penny-like question, despite the tightening in my chest: *What's the most scared you've ever been?*

My sternum frizzes after I ask the question, like it's warning me I should regret it, that I broke some social code, crossed some boundary. But Aarush only puts his pencil down and narrows his eyes in thought.

That's a good question, he says. He takes in a breath. For a moment I think he's going to avoid the question, and not want to answer. But he looks at me, exhales, and speaks like he trusts me. *Last year, the doctors thought my mom might have cancer. Luckily, what they found was benign. But before we knew she was gonna be okay, that was the most scared I've ever been.*

Grandma's still asleep in her chair, breathing deeply.

Wow, I say. *Yeah, that would be really scary.*

That's why I want to study medicine. I have to. If she ever got sick again . . .

I nod. I know what kind of scared he's talking about—the kind that makes everything you see, every tree and cloud and house, seem fake and insignificant compared to the awful thing happening. Compared to something like a loved one's declining heart.

For a second I have a jolt of worry that Aarush is going to

ask me the same question, but I turn back to the worksheet in front of me and he doesn't. I imagine telling him everything, telling him about the blank eyes and the Fear Maker and the sunflower garden. Aarush was so honest. He trusted me with this part of his story, so why is it so hard to trust him with mine? He seems all right with both helping others and asking for help. How does he do that without being terrified of something going horribly wrong? Of *doing* something horribly wrong?

Something horrible like trusting the monster under your bed?

What if I ask for help and the other person sees how weak and small I really am? What if I ask for help and it only ends up getting the other person hurt?

I wonder how many people the Fear Maker has already hit. I've only seen a few of the blank-eyed people, but that doesn't mean there aren't more. More stolen souls I haven't seen yet. What if he's getting more and more people every day? Getting closer and closer to the people I care about most?

But Aarush cares so much about medicine. What if he has ideas about healing blank eyes and devoured souls?

You know what, Aarush says. *You ask big questions. I like the way you think.*

Golden Spiral

I can't solve the equation
of saving lost souls.
My protective shells
keep turning into storm systems.

Who can sew a bag big enough
to collect all the lost souls?
Who is strong enough
to carry it? If I

take each one, place them all
on the sand in the shape
of a golden spiral,
will the tide wash them clean

and bring them home?

Mashed Potatoes

For Sunday dinner, we always lean in fully to the Idaho cliché and make a potato bar.

Roasties with oil and garlic. Mashed potatoes with their red skins still on and blended with piles of butter and sour cream. Baked potatoes with chives, and au gratin potatoes swimming in cheese.

Dad drives the twenty-seven minutes across town and picks up Grandma. We pull out the leaves around our table to make it bigger.

Mom, Dad, me, Grandma. And now Aarush, his mom, dad, and little brother.

We have to bring in extra chairs.

We have to use mismatched plates.

There are a lot of people. And somehow, I'm not as anxious about it as I thought I'd be. Maybe it's the warm potatoes and the warm laughs. Maybe it's the seeds I have in my pocket.

The adults arranged this get-together. Aarush's mom brings a crisp green salad and a yellow curry with chopped potatoes and carrots. The potato bar is complete.

It's been a few days since I've seen anyone with those nothing-eyes, although Mr. Reitman has been acting weirder and weirder, and we had a sub on Friday.

It's been a few days since the Garden. I've looked. I've set my alarm for six a.m., for five a.m., for three, any random time

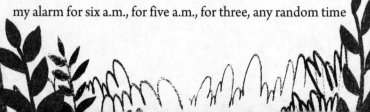

just to see if the Garden will come back, to see if I can find that light coming from behind my shower door again. I've checked first thing after school, and after dinner, too. Nothing.

I don't think I'll ever stop looking.

Hey, Dad? I say, as everyone sits with their plates piled high with potatoes. *How about today? Favorite flower?*

Hmm, he says. *Maybe not the best thing to think about during dinner, but I keep thinking about the corpse flower. I wonder if I'll ever get to see one. How about you?*

A potato flower, I say, grinning.

He laughs. *Poisonous, but much better smelling than my choice,* he says.

Usually Dad says something like dahlia or marigold, but I guess a human-sized flower that only blooms once every decade and smells like death would be pretty unique.

At dinner, I'm next to Aarush. Meals, I think, make communication easier because you can eat a spoonful of those mashed potatoes when you don't know what to say. But I guess with Aarush, I don't need to worry anyway, because even with his mouth full he talks. He says:

These potatoes are amazing!

For homeschool sometimes we do cooking lessons. Maybe I'll learn how to make these. It is Idaho after all.

So have you thought about the contest I sent you? What do you think?

I chew my potatoes slowly.

I chew my thoughts slowly.

These faces here are open. The adults are talking. Aarush's

dad is cutting something on his little brother Dev's plate. Again I imagine telling him about everything, about how nightmares and blank-eyed people are making it even harder for me to think about sending out my poems. And I think about telling him—telling all of them—about the sun-warm sunflower garden I found in my shower one morning.

The Garden—how could I bear having it disbelieved? Dismissed? I could not could not could not. That place is my place, and means too much to me to hear someone reject it, or treat it indifferently. The Garden is my pearl, and I have to keep it safe in my little clamshell.

How can I explain to Aarush that when I think of all the fear-making things, the nightmares, the house in the woods, the sick-grandma-hearts—the strangers' judgment slashing through my poems—it's like hundreds of those blank, blank eyes turning, oh so slowly, until they lock on me.

I swallow.

I don't know, I manage to say. *I'm not really ready.*

Aarush nods. *That's okay. Keep thinking about it. Let me know if you change your mind.*

Then we eat and eat, and eventually people start putting away food and clearing dishes. I'm standing next to Grandma and thinking about what she'd say if I told her everything, and about one of the poems in her book called "Tell Me Something I Don't Know."

Grandma?

Yes? she says.

Do you think . . . ? Do you believe things happen that we can't explain?

Grandma smiles, and with her round, knobby fingers tucks a bit of hair behind my ear.

Every day, she says. *I'm a poet, aren't I?*

So how do you know what's real and what isn't?

Grandma looks at me, her shoulders hunched, but her eyes as round and bright as forget-me-nots.

What do you *think?* she says.

Mashed Potatoes: A Poem

My sunflower brain
says, Have these mashed potatoes
with so much butter and
sour cream and garlic salt,
your friends and family
all around, mashed together,
warm warm warm.

My nightmare brain
says, Have these mashed potatoes
and good luck ignoring the rot
and swarming flies—
listen to the warm laughs now
because all these loved ones,
like the potatoes,
will soon be mine and
cold cold cold.

Worth a Thousand Pictures

I see Aarush a lot more over the next couple of weeks. He comes to my house and we work on homework or ride bikes, or we go to his house and play video games, and he keeps telling me that he likes my big questions and the way my brain works. I wonder if he'd still like it if he knew the full truth.

Then, on a crisp day in October, it's my time with Grandma again, and she and I take a trip.

Grandma squeezes my hand, grinning, as we look up at the bookshop. It's a brick building with tall windows. Our favorite place.

Be good, you two, says Mom, pulling away from the curb. In one hour, Mom will be back with a trunk full of groceries, and Grandma and I will have armfuls of books. Okay, maybe not literal armfuls, because books are expensive, and I think I only have enough money saved up for one, but my arms will carry around a nice big stack anyway while I decide which book to choose.

I'm wearing new shoes, too. Well, new to me. It turns out Aarush's mom has tiny feet and I have big feet and we are close enough to the same size that I can wear the lightly worn sneakers she wanted to give away. I'm not sure how she knew I needed them, but asking about it would just make me feel awkward. No more holes in the toe. For now.

At first I follow Grandma through the shelves, our fingertips trailing across the book spines like piano keys. As if by touching them, I can somehow absorb their stories and words and power.

After a minute, I drift toward the my-age books. I wonder if there are any about other kids who dream of Fear Makers and see blank-eyed, soul-sucked people when they wake. I find a book about a boy with a giant tree outside his bedroom window, and at night the tree turns into a monster and tells him stories. It looks promising, if not exactly like the stories the Fear Maker puts in my head at night.

But maybe I'm looking in the wrong place. I meander toward psychology and self-help. I see books about anxiety, books about dreaming, books about *Ten Ways to Build Your Self-Confidence!* None of them are quite what I need. None give me any hints about why I'm seeing what I'm seeing, or how to make the Fear Maker go far, far away, back to where he came from before I let him through the barrier between our world and his.

Then, like magnets slowly being pulled back together, Grandma and I find each other again in the poetry section. I realize I've been muttering some of my favorite lines from her poems to myself. I look at the wise, happy lines around Grandma's eyes. Maybe she's the person I should talk to. Would she know the answer—how to banish the Fear Maker? If I told her, would it make the white eyes and nighttime grips disappear? Or would it just make his waking-world power grow even stronger?

What did you find? Grandma says.

I show her the book about the tree monster.

Do you think monsters are real? I ask quietly. I've talked to her about monsters many times before, but never asked her this question so directly.

Grandma considers, closing the book she has in her hands. *Hmm,* she says. *I'm not sure. Possibly. But I do know that fighting monsters is* very real.

I'm not exactly sure what her answer means, but I like the way it sounds. Kind of like her poems. And I'm glad she didn't say outright that she didn't believe in monsters. Then what would I do? That would mean that everything—the nightmares, the Fear Maker, the blank eyes, even the Garden—was only in my mind, that I was falling off the edge of sanity. Then I could do nothing but not-golden spiral into dread dread dread.

What did you find? It's my turn to ask.

Grandma opens the book she's holding to the page her finger has marked. On one side is a photograph of three young men in suits and hats with farmland in the background, all looking at the camera. On the other side is a poem.

Have I taught you about ekphrastic poetry? Grandma says.

I shake my head.

Ekphrastic poems use someone's art, like a painting or sculpture or photograph like this one, as the whole basis for the poem. That's it, really, and you can take it in a thousand different directions. It's just a poem sort of describing the piece of art and how it makes you feel. Then you give your poem the same title as the art it's based on and voilà, ekphrastic poetry.

Ekphrastic. I roll the sound of the word around in my head. If that word was a person, I think they'd be a little excitable, a little nervous, a little bit wild. I think about the blue and black and yellow poster—another Van Gogh—that Grandma keeps above her reading chair. The way that painting, with that tall black spire looming in front of everything, seems to know exactly how it feels trying to see the world past all the nightmares the Fear Maker puts in front of you. I look at the sunflower painting on the cover of my notebook, each petal hanging on tight to brightness. I wonder if it would be possible to put into words what these paintings make me feel.

You could turn a lot of happy pictures into scary poems that way, I say.

Grandma nods. *Yes, absolutely. And scary pictures into happy poems, too.*

Sunflowers: An Ekphrastic

Flower heads look
every which way
and there's nothing still
about this life.

How many years—
how many failed attempts
and new mixtures
blending lights and darks

did it take to discover
how to make
an entire painting
out of nothing but

different shades of yellow?

After Mom and Dad Allow Me to Download a Video Chat App

Aarush (video from the back seat of his car): *You got the app! Woo-hoo! We're going to the alpaca sanctuary! I'll show you when we get there. Here's Dev. Say hi, Dev. And I was thinking about that contest thing; we could even make something cool of our own just for fun even if we didn't send it to the contest or anything. Oh, I think I see an alpaca! I think we're here! Okay, I'll send you a video from the alpacas. Welcome to Marco Polo!*

Me (from my backyard): *Um, hi, Aarush. This feels weird talking to the camera but seems fun, I guess. And definitely show me some alpacas. Um, well, this is my backyard. Those are the woods around my backyard and around the whole neighborhood. I don't really go in there that much. Or like, ever, really. They're not . . . fun woods. Um, yeah. Talk to you soon, I guess.*

Aarush (close up on an alpaca's face): *Look at that face! Look at those gnarly teeth! The lady said these ones don't really spit, though, so that's good. I think Dev's trying to get spit on. Those woods look awesome but definitely*

kinda spooky. Maybe you could write a poem about alpacas in spooky woods.

Me (from the kitchen): *So, um, I'm just in the kitchen now. I'm eating grapes and peanut butter. Have you ever tried that? It's like a tiny PB and J. It's good with Nutella, too. Anyway, um, that alpaca looks so cool. I'm not sure if I could write a poem about alpacas. I don't know what I'd say, but maybe I can try. I bet my grandma could do it. Um, give the alpacas a pat from me. Don't get spit on. Um, bye.*

Aarush (back in the car): *Okay, that was awesome! No spitting. Oh, I think we're getting frosted lemonade now, but I'll have to try the grapes and Nutella thing, that sounds yum. And heck yes, your grandma could write a poem about anything. I bet you could, too. Maybe I'll try drawing an alpaca. Show me your poem when you write it.*

Me (from my bedroom): *Only if you show me your drawing. Frosted lemonade sounds yum.*

Aarush (sipping lemonade): *It really is yum. Tag you're it.*

Me (from my room): *Tag you're it.*

Aarush (from his room): *Tag you're it.*

Me (from the front porch, at sunset): *Tag you're it.*

Aarush (from under the covers): *Okay, Mom says I have to put my phone away for tonight and go to bed, but tag you're it.*

Text from me (10:03 p.m.): Tag you're it.

Aarush (7:17 a.m.): Cheater.

What Did You Do at School Today?

On Monday my inside-tank is still pretty full up with the warmth of messages from Aarush and bookstore trips with Grandma. My steps are one beat less slow.

While I wait between classes, I watch the vid that Aarush sent me that morning, his bedhead hair smooshed up on one side.

Gooooood morning, Penny Hope! So I had this dream where you and me were riding a giant alpaca on the freeway? Like, we were just holding on to the alpaca's neck and going, like, seventy miles an hour and that was it. That was the whole dream. Weird, huh? Anyway have a good day at school. Don't let geometry get you down. Don't ride off on any animals without me.

I don't usually start Mr. Reitman's class smiling, but today I do. My backpack is set down under my feet. My notebook is out, and the lines I've written today . . . well, they're not terrible. There are even some math problems I understood—me, Penny Hope—and maybe this Mr. Reitman brand of weird isn't *that* weird. This feeling that he's acting even more different, that he's somehow not himself, could just be me.

My gaze is one little notch higher. I notice that the girl with mismatched socks has braces with light blue bands and a yellow scrunchie in her hair. When I small-firefly-flicker smile at her, she smiles back.

The classroom door opens. Loud.

Mr. Reitman steps in, laughing.

He looks around at all of us.

Everyone else just smiles.

They're looking up at the board, up at his face, not reacting. Smiling like nothing's wrong.

Even though Mr. Reitman's eyes are nothing-caverns: pockets of empty empty empty.

And I know I'm the only one who sees it.

Magic Tricks

Come here, Penny.
Want to see a magic trick?
I can make you
disappear.

Drive Drive Drive

Mr. Reitman stands there at the front of the class, his blank, nothing-eyes looking over us. When his gaze reaches me, he pauses a little longer. As if he can sense that I'm the one with the Fear Maker seed in my gut.

People around me pull out their notebooks and pencils like everything's normal. The girl in mismatched socks taps her eraser and hums a tune I don't know.

For the entire class, I'm frozen in my seat, white-knuckle gripping the sides of my chair. Shaking like there's a rickety wooden roller coaster climbing up a steep hill in my stomach.

Mr. Reitman looks at me and grins. I swear the Fear Maker is grinning somewhere, too.

Mr. Reitman writes the formula for calculating circumference on the board. He watches us, looking down his nose like a hawk, his shoulders and movements stiff and robotic. The people next to me are taking notes, but all I can think about are those eyes, the way his voice starts sounding odd and metallic and too even, as if the Fear Maker's gone now, gone entirely, leaving nothing but a Mr. Reitman shell. I try not to tremble out of my seat.

It didn't work. Rearranging my room, moving my bed away from the corner where I let the Fear Maker in all those years ago, even the poems and seeds. It didn't work. What else can I possibly do?

Mr. Reitman, when he was his normal self, said that triangles were the strongest shape, each of the three sides leaning on and supporting the others. I've got three things on my protection table—poems, pennies, seeds—so is one of those things not as lucky or strong as the others? Not doing what it's supposed to? Or is my table idea nonsense and I need to think of something else?

But what? And even if I can think of something else to try, what if it's not enough?

Whatever it is, I have to figure it out before the Fear Maker takes over everyone everyone everyone.

I sit there gripping, clenching every muscle until my arms ache. My papers and pencils never make it out of my backpack—Mr. Reitman never says anything about it; he just looks at me and grins wider—so when the bell finally rings, I grab my backpack and run. Run right past the tray where I'm supposed to turn in my homework, and out the door.

After school I am ready to crumble, ready to crawl under my big quilt, so I run to Mom's car as soon as she pulls into the pickup line. I pull on my seat belt and hold it till my knuckles are white. I want to tell my mom to just keep going, to just drive and drive and drive away from here.

What a pile of hours it is, the time driving home from school.

How was school today? Mom asks.

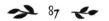

Her eyes are on the road ahead. (Normal eyes. I checked first thing.) There's that worry line across her forehead like a canyon. I want to tell her. The words to explain the blank eyes are thick and sticky like toffee, hard to chew, but maybe I could try. Maybe I could explain about eating the Fear Maker's treat and letting him in all those years ago. Maybe I could tell her about what I really found the day I went into the woods, and how just remembering the way it felt seeing that house in real life makes my fingers freeze so bad I can hardly hold my pen properly. Maybe I could explain about the grip from under the bed, how I keep seeing people with the color sucked out of their eyes. How I keep *not* seeing the light from the Garden, where everything is okay. Maybe I could tell her, and maybe she'd believe me. Maybe it's time. But Mom speaks first.

Honey, she says. *I need to talk to you about something.*

Okay. I pull back the words I was about to say. It's probably best Mom spoke first, and I can tell from her furrowed brow that this is serious.

It's not bad news, she adds. *It's just tricky. Different.*

She keeps looking ahead and puts her shoulders back like she's practiced these words over and over.

With Grandma at the assisted living home, the financial situation is a little tighter than we thought. You already know that. Olympus is wonderful and Grandma is well taken care of there, but especially with things being slow at the shop lately, it's tough.

She swallows. Clears her throat.

So Dad and I have agreed that I'm going to start looking at possible job options. Not quite sure what's going to happen yet, and Dad wasn't thrilled about me giving up volunteering at the library because he knows how much I love it. But I just have to focus on finding full-time work. And it's too bad . . . I did ask at the library, but there just aren't any jobs there right now.

But I'm sure this will all be for the best. I've actually got a job interview tomorrow. Mrs. Banerjee agreed to pick you up from school, and instead of going to Grandma's, you can hang out at Aarush's house for an hour or so.

I'm silent as Mom continues. Do you understand? This will hopefully mean we can do things like buy you new shoes, not just depend on hand-me-downs. She pauses. I know this is a lot, she says. Are you going to be okay?

Mom is glancing at me.

Thump-thump goes the road as we drive.

It's like speed chess in my brain, trying to figure out how to respond. What do I say?

For a moment I was ready to tell her everything—all about the Fear Maker and the Garden—but that moment is gone. Somehow, trying to talk about my nightmares seems so . . . hazy, after the solid, heavy reality of what Mom just said. Of what she's dealing with. Like trying to put a rain cloud on a platter next to the mashed potatoes. And I keep coming back to this: What can Mom do about the blank eyes, anyway? Even if she believed me, she can't see them. Can't see my nightmares. Talking about blank eyes and sunflower gardens will just distract her from focusing on her own task ahead of her. She needs to focus on finding work and helping us keep afloat, and I will focus on finding my Garden, because that feels like the most likely place to find the answers to the Fear Maker problem. And because not ever finding my Garden again would cost me much more than money.

So I find a different truth to say.

You'll be great, Mom.

My grip on the seat belt tightens.

Turning on the Lights

I was seven and in my dad's flower shop.

It was a few weeks after Halloween. After that night with the apple. The nightmares had begun, and my body had started feeling different, like the seed I'd swallowed had nestled inside me, finding a place in the lining of my stomach. The Fear Maker taking root in me.

Post-Halloween is poinsettia season in the flower shop. There was fresh, fluffy Idaho snow on the ground outside, and new bouquets of bursting red flowers that Dad and I had just finished setting up all around the shop. It was a little past closing time, and the sky outside was inky fleece. The deep expanse of a night sky wasn't something I'd really noticed before, until that Halloween. I noticed it that night, like a scratchy cloak getting heavier on my skin.

But Dad was there, so at least I wasn't alone.

They were used to me being their helper. Their *right-hand woman* was what Mom called me.

I helped make signs and water flowers and set up displays in the shop.

I helped make orange rolls and gingerbread houses and art projects in the kitchen.

Because, to be honest, up to then, I probably would have thrown a tantrum if they *didn't* let me help.

Seven-year-old Penny, Daddy's helper in his flower shop,

and it was time to finish the last display of Christmas flowers. He even let me help make the Christmas playlist that would gently welcome customers when they walked in.

He stood by the entrance, looking over our new wintry setup.

This is wonderful, Dad said, hands on his hips. *I think it just needs one more strand of twinkle lights up at this front table here. There should be another box in the storage closet. Can you go get that, sweetie, while I close out the register?*

Twinkle lights from the storage closet? I could do that.

I booked it around the displays, around the counter, turned the corner, and scooted down the hall. I was always excited to help, always excited for more twinkle lights. The closet was past the bathrooms and the cold storage room and around yet another corner, where the light from the hallway didn't reach quite as well.

I stood facing the storage door.

I'd done this a hundred times before, gone to the storage closet by myself. So why was I hesitating? Why was the pit in my stomach rolling and crashing against my ribs?

Because the only way to turn on the closet light was to step through a long room of shadows. The light was all the way at the back, one hanging bulb turned on by one flimsy string dangling to the floor.

I'd never thought twice about going into the closet before, but now, with each blink, I imagined new horrors I might find, and the images shot cold adrenaline through my belly.

I imagined rats scurrying and cockroaches crawling up my legs.

I imagined turning on the light and seeing severed hands lining the shelves.

Walking into shadows, tugging on the light, and finding myself face-to-face with the man from my nightmares: a tall man in the corner with glowing red eyes and quick, grabbing hands.

And as I stood there, staring at the closed door, I could have sworn I saw the shadow of a long, thin hand pass across its surface. Or was it my imagination? When I blinked, it was gone, and I was left trembling.

When Dad found me, my feet were stuck to the floor like tree roots, my face was streaming wet with tears, and my lungs gasped and clutched, trying to get enough air.

What's wrong? he asked. *What happened, sweetie?*

I couldn't answer. I couldn't breathe.

Dad picked me up and held me close until I stopped heaving. He carried me out to the car and talked to me about snow and poinsettias all the way home.

Mom made me orange rolls and hot cocoa while Dad whispered to her about what had happened. I think this was the night they realized that something had changed. I was still shaking with terror, but also embarrassed. Even though some of the Fear Maker nightmares had started by then, they'd never hit me in the real-life stomach like that before. Never stopped me from helping, from going into the closet and turning on the light.

I felt like I was watching the Penny I knew lose her petals one by one.

Back to Before

How can autumn leaves be
pasted back to branches,
turned green again?

Can a rusted, rubbed-out penny
be scrubbed clean
and reminted like new?

Where's the time machine to take me
back to a self I recognize, before
the monster's teeth took a chunk of me

right from the middle?

Not Here

Before dinner, before sunset and nighttime, I walk the loop around our neighborhood. Past the mailboxes, the street-parked flatbed trucks, the big house at the end of the road with the dark green shutters. I'm looking for a flicker, any glimpse at all of that yellow Garden light. It hasn't shown back up in the bathroom or anywhere else in the house, and I'm getting desperate. Maybe it will reappear somewhere else? Wherever it is, I have to find it. I can be safe there. I can find a way to keep my family safe there. But I can't find it anywhere.

We eat leftover potatoes for dinner. Besides wandering the neighborhood, I also spend an hour in the bathroom—if I wait long enough, maybe the Garden will come back—until Mom knocks, worried.

You okay, sweetie?

Just thinking, I say.

You sure everything's all right?

I flush the toilet, pretending I've been in the bathroom for normal reasons, and even wash my hands before I open the door, trying a light smile like nothing's really that wrong.

Yep, I'm fine. Just a thinky night.

Okay, Mom says, though she still looks a bit concerned. *Tell me if you need anything.*

She goes back to reading in the front room with Dad, and while they think I'm getting ready for bed, I search. I softly, quietly open every drawer in the kitchen, who knows why, really. I tiptoe to the basement and stare hard at the cellar door, willing it to glow. I check the guest room—Grandma's old room—and the guest room closet. When I'm sure my parents aren't looking, I peek into their room, too.

The sun is gone and I know it's going to be bedtime soon. It's going to be me alone in my room, time to turn out the lights. The trees seem closer than ever.

I need the Garden more than ever.

The shadows are going to drown me.

I need the Garden. Now.

And it is.

Not.

Here.

Alone

The last yellow
leaf on the tree—
does it cling tight
or wish it could fall?
<u>Rain clouds are coming,</u>
the cold wind whispers,
but no one listens.
Little yellow leaf,
do you feel alone
too?

Turn Around

This time, in this nightmare, I'm throwing up.

This time, when I walked through the Fear Maker's front door, I found another city, this one raucous and frantic and deafening.

I'm in a huge, jostling crowd with giant skyscrapers and jumbotrons on every side, lights spinning, a haunted-circus type of Times Square. And in the middle of this crashing tide of people, I'm bent over, vomiting.

Except it's not puke—I'm throwing up my teeth. They fall out of my mouth one by one, but when they clatter onto the cement, they're glinting copper coins.

I'm throwing up pennies.

And they keep coming. Pennies pour and pour out of my mouth and nobody notices. The crowd keeps roiling around me, and as I vomit pennies I see myself start to disappear, from my feet upward. My color evaporates, then my feet are gone, my shins, my knees, my belly—like the pennies I'm throwing up are myself, and I can't stop.

I watch my hands, my arms, and the rest of myself vanish until there's nothing but my invisible self and the pile of copper pennies on the ground that everyone is ignoring.

Someone, help. Please.

I test my voice.

Help. Help.

It comes out in a whisper, but it does come.

Help. Help me.

Louder. Louder this time until I'm screaming.

Nobody hears me. All the people flow around me, none of them seeing or listening.

I push through them like a salmon swimming upstream. They jostle as I bump and shove them, but their eyes see past me, through me, and they don't hear me no matter how loud I scream. Not even if I shout in their faces.

A voice speaks from one of the jumbotrons. Somehow the voice is both amplified and right behind me. It's that voice I recognize. If I turn around, I know, I just know, I'll see a shadow face with red eyes on the big screen.

It's your fault, Penny, he says.

It's all your fault.

He doesn't say what *it* is, because *it* means *everything*.

Just turn around and I'll fix it.

Just turn around. I'll fix everything and leave.

Then I see them, up ahead. Mom and Dad.

Mom! Dad! I scream, and run forward.

I'm nearly to them. I could almost reach out past the line of people between us and touch Dad's shoulder, but the line of people will not budge.

Mom! Dad! Help me!

I scream and scream until my disappeared throat feels like a wound.

I scream, and the crowd keeps moving, Mom and Dad with them.

Behind me, the voice is laughing.

I wake up.

Mirror Mirror on the Wall

I wake up hyperventilating, my throat clutching. Again. A strand of hair is plastered to my sweaty, clammy cheek. I can still hear that laughing ringing in my head. Still see Mom and Dad walking away as I scream for them.

My body has to move. Stepping as far away from the bed as I can (not risking another grip on my ankle, ever, ever again), I stumble out into the hall and to the bathroom. This routine of trying and failing to wash nightmare off my face is wearing me ragged.

A sip of water. A splash under the eyes. But when I look up, the mirror is fogged, as if a hot shower had been running.

And in the steamed-up mirror, a word forms. A word written by an unseen finger.

Delicious.

I feel the terror in my blood run hot enough that I could combust.

It takes every bit of control I have not to scream.

Because what if screaming only brings the Fear Maker closer than he already is?

How Much Does a Day Weigh?

It's Tuesday morning. Dad's at the shop. Mom sets cereal on the table, checks her email, distracted and nervous about the interview she has later.

I want to speak. Last night feels like too much weight to bear on my own, and I want to tell her about the laughing nightmare and the message in the mirror even if the moment is never right. I want to tell her I can't go to school, can't bear Mr. Reitman looking at me with those nothing-eyes, but the words don't come.

I haven't interviewed in over a decade, Mom says.

I can't tell her, can't say I'm sick and need to stay home, not when she's dealing with such a big thing already. I try to keep the shiver from my voice and tell her she'll do great, and she doesn't notice the cracks in my words, in my breath. But I know that's just because she's stressed to the limit and focused on everything she has to do. Right?

So that's how I end up at school, walking in like Red into the wolf's mouth. Like Frodo into Mordor.

I know what's waiting for me. I try to step step step across the squeaky tiles. Those eyes are waiting for me. Kids flow around me. Paper skeletons, crepe pumpkins, and other Halloween decorations twirl from the ceiling and wink at me from the walls. A boy with a big gray backpack bumps me on the shoulder. The closer I get to the classroom, the harder it is to walk.

The hall smells like peanut butter and Pine-Sol. My feet are cement blocks and the crowd around me thins to a trickle until it's just me alone in the hallway. The bell must've rung, even though I didn't hear it. I think about messaging Aarush, but right now I don't know what I'd say.

Someone will find me soon. A teacher or hall monitor. I can't just stand here. Because what kind of person would find me? A regular teacher, or someone with the blank, blank eyes, staring at me down the hallway? Someone with an eaten, devoured soul?

I see it in my mind, think of sitting in class, sitting at that wooden desk with the scratches on the front while Mr. Reitman looks at me.

I run.

Run run run, down the hall, around a corner, past lockers and classrooms. I don't really see where I'm going, but I need somewhere to hide. There's a collapsing earthquake along my sternum and I can't breathe. My vision narrows, shadows creeping in at the edges.

And then somehow I'm by the janitor's closet.

And the door is glowing.

The Gardener

The light—I want to drink it in, and I want to run through this field and wrap my arms around as many sunflowers as I possibly can, let the sticky, earthy scent fill me up to the brain. The soil is so soft and rich, the kind you want to get down and run your fingers through.

So I kneel and reach my fingers into the dirt up to my knuckles. I wish I could plant myself here. For a moment I do feel planted, the earth below and the sun above pouring in through that tender spot at the top of my skull.

My sunflowers are back.

As if, somehow, I dove into the painting on the cover of my notebook and found a whole world. Or maybe the world found me again.

My laughter is the color of the sky. A breeze runs its fingers through my hair in response, blowing the rising tears from my face. I stand up, not bothering to brush the dirt off my knees, and I walk and walk and think this must be how a lizard feels after it's sloughed off its grimy, itching, cracking, wrong-fitting skin.

I follow the path, which follows me. I imagine this whole place, all this earth, as a giant quilt that I could pull up over my shoulders, tuck under my chin, sunflowers poking out at the elbows. There are more colors in the petals and the sky than I

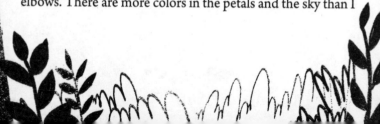

noticed at first. Different shades along the rims of clouds and the edges of petals, rich layers I only catch when I look closely.

After walking for a while—a walk, it feels, back into myself—I think of my pale green bench. And then there it is.

With someone sitting on it.

The someone is a broad-shouldered man with vivid red hair and a scruffy beard. He looks about my dad's age, maybe a bit younger. He has a long, bumped nose and wears a large brown coat and straw hat. For a split second I'm taken off guard, wondering what someone else is doing in my safe place. But after a moment of looking at him, I get the sense that he was here first, and has been here all along.

If the Fear Maker seems to suck away joy and peace like a void, this man is the opposite. He emanates rich warmth, like the sunflowers themselves. This rugged, luminous man seems to belong there on the bench, and by the way he looks at the nearest petals, the way he tilts his head up to the sky, I know this is his Garden—his safe place—too.

At first I'm not sure if he notices me. I'm about to walk away and find another bench and not bother him, but then he speaks.

"Penelope Hope," he says. "Come look at this beautiful fellow."

He is pointing at something on top of one of the flowers, where a butterfly is perched. I step closer and see swirling red and blue in its wings.

Then the man stands, turns to me, and smiles. His face is

clear and wholehearted, filling me up instead of draining me down, the way the Fear Maker does with his cold, tight grin. This man's eyes are swirling layers of blue and all the brightest sky colors. He reaches out a hand, a big hand, and shakes mine. His hand is warm and there is dirt under his fingernails that matches mine.

"Penelope Hope." He says my name again, like he's making sure I know he knows I'm there, and he sees me. "It is a pleasure to meet you. I'm the Gardener."

Questions

"You know who I am?" I ask.

The Gardener laughs, jolly, his big shoulders bouncing. "Yes. And I know there's been a lot going on. I know you've been dealing with terrifying things all on your own. I know the feeling."

I feel the validation of his words like coming in from a cold night to a crackling, soothing fire. He moseys down the path and soon we're walking through the sunflowers shoulder to shoulder, as if we've walked like this three thousand times before. As natural as that time my family went to the tulip festival in Oregon, where there was a red wooden windmill, and my dad scooped me up and put me on his shoulders. Here, that memory is clear and strong.

I have so many questions. The Gardener is quiet, patient as I reach for the right words. Each question is a seed to plant, and I don't know where to start.

"What is this place?" I ask. The most straightforward question, perhaps.

"This is the Garden," he says simply.

"Why couldn't I find it before? When I needed it."

"But you *did* find it," he says. "When you need it the very most, when things are the most desperate, you'll find it." A dragonfly with stained-glass wings lifts off from its perch on a nearby sunflower stem and pirouettes around the Gardener's head, and he smiles. I hadn't noticed the birds and the insects till I was with him. Still, bits of my questions linger. Wasn't I desperate before? Didn't I need the Garden before? Is there something larger at play, bigger than I can see? Those questions don't go away, but here with the Gardener they feel easier to carry, and ultimately, he's right. I *did* find the Garden again.

Part of me wants to not ask my next questions, to ignore them and pretend I can just stay here forever. But I know that's not true, and I know if I can't ask the Gardener, I can't ask anyone.

"The people ... the eyes ... can you see them, too? It's because of the Fear Maker, isn't it? Like in my nightmares?"

The Gardener looks at me then, his thick brow furrowed with worry and his blue eyes so sad.

"I'm so sorry you have to deal with this," he says. "I wish you didn't. Yes, the people with blank eyes are the ones whose souls have been taken by the Fear Maker. He uses the souls to build his house in the woods. Or feed it. Both words mean the same thing when it comes to that place."

"But ... back home, I still see those people, except with empty eyes. So what happened to them? Are they still ... there inside? Themselves?"

"Good question," the Gardener says. "He takes what's inside, their Them-ness, and leaves the rest. What's left goes through the motions, goes through the routine, like a shell moving along grooves in the sand without the creature inside. What you're seeing is that shell."

I nod. Somehow this seems like something I already knew. It fits what I've seen both awake and asleep. And somehow, I trust the Gardener's answers. I trust him the way I trust Grandma, the way I've come to trust Aarush. There's no hint of the deceit and betrayal I've been afraid of since my seven-year-old self thought she could be nice to a monster, to the Fear Maker. That kind of malice doesn't seem possible here, in this Garden. I believe the Gardener when he says he wants to help and wishes I didn't have to go through all this.

"The Fear Maker lives in that . . . that clearing I went to, once," I say. "I can feel his house growing. Like the seed in my stomach."

"Yes," says the Gardener, nodding. "That connection, from that night—that is real. Tangible."

"That's why I can feel him getting stronger. Feel my fear getting stronger."

The Gardener swallows, looking like he's about to cry. "Yes," he says.

"Is that why I'm the only one who sees him?" This—this lonely, desperate question is the one I really want to ask, and it cracks through my voice when I whisper, "Why can't other people see the blank eyes?"

As he answers, the Gardener's shoulders are hunched, like he's carrying a heavy sack across his back. His voice is quiet. "There is not just one Fear Maker, Penny Hope. There are many. So many. Each one is different. Some look human, some don't. There are big ones and small ones. There's a Fear Maker for every person. A Fear Maker that lives in nightmares and the murkiest corners of each person's thoughts." The Gardener pauses, looking at the worry and amazement that must be written across my forehead. "This Fear Maker is yours."

We walk slowly as I take in this information. I'm grateful for the sun and the ocean of flowers that seems to be buoying me along. I can't tell if this is comforting news, or if it makes things worse. Because on the one hand, knowing that there is a Fear Maker for each person means I'm not alone. It means I'm not abnormal. Not a freak. If this is my Fear Maker, it makes sense that other people might notice something's off, but I'm the only one who actually sees the vacant eyes.

On the other hand, if everybody has a Fear Maker of their own, why is mine able to touch other people and steal their Them-ness? Why is mine the one leaving me messages not just in nightmares, but in the real world? Why is mine the one running amok, snatching souls to feed his hungry house?

I'm about to ask the Gardener these questions, but I realize I already know the answers.

"And mine got tangible power in our world because of the candy I left under my bed, and because of the caramel apple," I say.

A breeze ruffles the lapels on the Gardener's coat. "The barrier between us and our nightmares is thinnest on Halloween nights. When he came knocking on the other side, your offering thinned the barrier even more, and your Fear Maker took advantage. He betrayed your generosity and your bravery and your kindness."

"I don't feel very brave," I say immediately, a knee-jerk

reaction. "And now it's my Fear Maker that's doing all this, my fault for—"

"Penelope Hope, I need you to understand something very important. Are you listening?"

I nod, wanting to bury my head in his coat or lie down covered in sunflowers and escape everything.

He puts a gentle hand on my shoulder, and as I look at his eyes it seems like the blue sky is pouring into me. "You didn't do anything wrong," he says. "Kindness is never wrong. You are brave and strong and good. You have the courage to fight this Fear Maker. Everything you need—it's all inside you already."

"But how? How do I fight him?"

"Ah," the Gardener says. "That brings me to a question I have for *you*. Is that all right?"

I nod. I realize that I've had an entire conversation without feeling that self-conscious twinge that keeps me looking down, and without ever worrying about what to say. Somehow I feel more safe and natural in my own skin talking to the Gardener than I ever have before, even with my parents or Aarush. It's a refreshing feeling.

"It's a big question," the Gardener says. "There's an important task ahead of you. Your Fear Maker—his strength and hold in your world is growing. I know you've sensed that. Banishing him from your world won't be an easy fight. But the big battle is not here yet. For now, a smaller undertaking. Something that might help you prepare. Will you do something for me? Will you do one thing—pick one thing you're afraid to do, and do it?"

"Does this mean I'll see you again?" I say, without really thinking.

The Gardener laughs. "Yes. Yes, you will."

Then the rest of what he said registers. One thing I'm afraid to do. In here, there's nothing I couldn't handle, but out there—out there, there are so many. I want to jump and say yes, and here in these flowers I think I could. But back out there, with the nightmares and the Fear Maker?

Now it's my turn to swallow hard.

"I'll try," I say.

"That's all I ask," says the Gardener.

We walk a little while longer, this time in silence and thought. One scary thing. One thing, like one line in a poem against nightmares, like Grandma suggested. I think of my scribbled poems in my notebook, and I know what scary thing I need to do. It's a small thing in here, but Out-There-Penny will be terrified.

Ahead is the little cottage with the wooden door. The door back to my world, where I must figure out how to beat a monster. "It's time for me to leave now, isn't it?" I ask.

"For now," says the Gardener.

We take a few steps toward the door and I put my hand on the knob.

"Mr. Gardener?" I say.

"Yes?"

"How do you know so much about the Fear Maker?"

The Gardener's face, which seemed young a moment ago, is now tinted with the shadows of old scars and deep lines, and

I know this is not the first monster the Gardener has faced. If I could dive into his eyes, and if I went deep enough, perhaps I'd reach a time when this Garden was empty and bleak, bleak as my nightmares, scorched beyond life, beyond any hope of seeds sprouting ever again. But they did sprout. Sprouted big and bright and yellow clear out to the horizon.

Then the Gardener steps toward me, his first step the tiniest limp, but he eases into his sunflower-garden stride and pulls me into a tight hug, his arms wrapped all the way around me. His arms are strong and he smells of wet earth and coffee grounds.

"Here," he says, stepping back and reaching into one of the pockets of his coat. He pulls out a fist and then drops a big palmful of sunflower seeds into my outstretched hand.

"Take these with you," he says.

I put the seeds into my jacket pocket. I don't want to say goodbye, and it doesn't seem the right thing to do anyway. So without saying anything, I face the cottage door, square my shoulders, and turn the knob.

Seeds

Hand cupped around the seeds in my pocket, I make it through school. I make it to math class just four minutes late, and I take my seat and Mr. Reitman watches me but says nothing.

When Mr. Reitman looks at me, I look back at him. I don't know how, but I do, and I don't think the Fear Maker likes it. The seeds are smooth and warm under my fingers and I look back into those blank eyes that are looking at me while Mr. Reitman teaches us about acute angles. He doesn't call on me once during the whole class. When he isn't looking, Mismatched Socks Girl gives me an eye roll and a smile like *isn't this the worst*, and even though she doesn't see what I see, I smile and sigh in return.

Aarush and his mom are there in the pickup line when the last bell rings. Now that I've been in their car and at their house a few times, even my bones feel grateful for the familiarity. Something recognizable where I can relax a little bit, after clenching on to every ounce of courage I could muster all day long.

I close the door behind me like I'm hopping into a getaway car, but I made it. Today, at least, I made it. When I take my hand out of my pocket and relax my grip, I realize I've been clutching at the seeds all day and their shapes are printed into my palm.

We get to Aarush's house and have samosas for snacks, then milk and Oreos. *For a well-rounded meal*, says Mrs. Banerjee.

Aarush tells me about a place he and his mom and brother went to that taught them how to spin clay pots and bowls. He takes me to his room and shows me the slightly lopsided bowl he made, with a chevron-shaped pattern lining the outside.

Now that it's just me and Aarush, it's time to tell him about my plan. The Gardener asked me to do something scary, and I think I know exactly what that something is.

Hey, I say. *I'll do it. I'll do the poetry contest.*

You will? he says, bouncing. *Excellent!*

Aarush goes to his desk and opens a drawer of neatly stacked notebooks and papers. If I opened his closet, I wonder if all his button-down shirts would be color sorted.

I was imagining something a little . . . ominous. A little frightening, I say, thinking of all the poems I have in my sunflower notebook.

Oooh, yes, he says. *I mean, it's October anyway.*

He snaps his fingers, like a thought just clicked into place, then he scurry-flurries through his drawer and takes out a large drawing pad. He flips through page after page until he finds the right one.

Something like this? he says. He turns the drawing toward me.

The drawing is of a house in the night. There's a rickety porch, an empty rocking chair, and closed shutters, which make the house seem as if at any moment, it will open its window eyes and wake up. There's a huge, leafless tree hanging over the page, nearly twice as tall as the house itself. The branches and twigs look like they're tapping finger bones, like they're moving.

The house from my nightmares.

It's like my stomach is a bucket and someone just filled it with ice water. How is this possible? It takes a few seconds to even process what I'm seeing.

Have you . . . have you seen this house before?

Well . . . Aarush says, hesitant, which is unusual for him. But then he looks at me and smiles. *Okay, this is going to sound weird, but I saw it in a dream, and my great-grandfather was showing me this house and I don't remember what he said, just that he sounded worried, like he was telling me to be careful. Then I woke up and drew this. That probably sounds totally stupid.*

I stare at the drawing. Aarush's great-grandfather showed him the Fear Maker's house in a dream? That thought tingles in my spine. I have no clue what to make of it or what it means—does it mean Aarush is in extra danger? Does it mean, maybe, that he's especially prepared to help me?

I carefully touch the sketched tree, like the branches might reach off the page and prick my finger.

Not stupid at all, I say. *And yeah, I can definitely do something with this.*

Awesome, says Aarush. *I'll get working on turning this idea into a painting. It'll be even cooler that way, and with your poem! Because I know it's going to be great!*

His confidence makes my face warm and I hope I don't let him down. I'm trying, Mr. Gardener, I think to myself.

Aarush tosses the notebook onto his bed, then follows it himself, flopping and mussing the neatly tucked covers. I take a seat in the desk chair.

What changed your mind? he asks.

That's a question. *The* question.

I think about the Gardener. I think of all the other things that can change minds. Friends. Moms and dads. Math equations. Hunger, nightmares, poems. Sunflower seeds.

I wonder if it's time to tell someone the truth—tell Aarush the truth. An experiment, to see how he reacts. My parents not believing me? I think I'd crumble, collapse in on myself like a house-swallowing sinkhole. But this boy with his ties and neatly parted hair and open, open eyes . . . it would be a relief beyond words to be believed. To not be alone in this.

Now that I've said yes to the contest, what else might I say yes to? Maybe that yes, a yes to Aarush, a yes to a friend, is a seed, and something might grow in me. Maybe not a garden—not yet—but something. And after what he told me about his dream, maybe he won't think my story is completely, utterly, entirely unreal.

You really want to know why I changed my mind? I say.

Of course. Did something happen?

I nod. *It's happening now,* I say. *It's going to sound completely impossible, but it's real. I'm going to tell you the truth, okay?*

Okay, he says seriously, like he knows what this means, how big a deal it is, what I'm about to tell him.

And I do. I tell him the truth. I start with the monster under the bed, leaving him candy, and eating the caramel apple. I tell him about the nightmares, the people acting strange, the blank, soul-sucked eyes that nobody else sees. I tell him about, once, going into the woods to find the Fear Maker's house and how I still see it in my nightmares, growing. I tell him about Mr. Reitman. I tell him about the voice that laughs in the night and the hands getting closer. I tell him about the Fear Maker.

Then I tell him about the light. The yellow light. I tell him about stumbling, desperate, into the Garden.

Aarush's eyes get bigger and bigger, and I tell him about the sunflowers, all the millions of sunflowers, and, lastly, the Gardener, who knew my name and told me I was brave.

That house? The house you drew? That's the Fear Maker's house. The one I saw in the woods, only it was smaller back then. I have no idea how you dreamed about it, if your great-grandfather is warning you or something else is happening or what, but the Gardener told me about all the souls trapped there, feeding his house, and that fighting the Fear Maker will be a hard battle and I need to prepare. For now, he asked me to do one thing, just one thing I'm afraid of, which is why I changed my mind about the contest. And he gave me these.

I reach out my hand, and Aarush, uncharacteristically silent, does too. Sometime while I was talking I stood and walked over to him without really thinking. Standing there in the middle of his room, I pour half my pocketful of sunflower seeds into his palm. He stares. He runs a finger over them, counting them.

Seven, he says. *My lucky number.*

You can keep them, I say. It feels important to say it.

Then quiet. Waiting. Still don't know what he thinks, if he's going to run away from me, if he—

I believe you, he says.

He looks between his palmful of seeds and my face. I read a whole novel in his eyes. He spoke the words quickly, maybe too quickly, and now his thoughts are catching up to him. I see him questioning his own mind, like I did. I see him flip through question after question, thought after thought. Does he actually believe me? Is the story I just told him a trick? A figment of my fevered imagination? Or is it a truth stranger than nightmares? Then, in his face, a firmness appears. Determination.

Yes. I believe you.

I blink, a current of warm electricity in my bones.

You do? I ask.

He looks up at me, mouth open like he's still fitting my story into his mind. *There's a story, a story my family tells every Diwali. About my great-grandfather. The one from my dream. My seventh great-grandfather, actually. I'm even named after him. The story starts when he had absolutely nothing, no family, no food, and was ready to give up and lie in his bed until Yama was ready for him—except that night he had a dream. In the dream he was chasing a crow who had seven seeds in its beak. The crow landed out of reach, and planted the first seed in the ground. Just as my great-grandfather was about to catch him, the crow flew off, before landing and planting the second seed. This happened again, and again, until the seventh seed was planted, and just as he was about to catch the crow, he woke up.*

Aarush touches the seeds with one finger, gently spreading them around his palm.

The next morning, following the dream, my great-grandfather used the last of his energy to walk into the forest outside his village. On his way he passed a tall banyan tree he'd never seen before, then another. At the seventh banyan tree, something glittering on the ground caught his eye. He found seven coins, enough to buy food and passage to the city, where he went to school and became a teacher.

My friend looks up at me, his face bright with wonder. It seems I'm not the only one to experience that foggy area where dreams and reality blend together. Maybe having that story in his family helped him understand my story. That bit of me that Aarush has now. Maybe that's what it really means to become friends with someone. We know each other's stories now. We're *in* each other's stories now.

I don't know what my dream means exactly, either . . . why I dreamed about him showing me that house, but my mom says the ancestors are still watching out for us and know what's going on. He holds the seeds tightly. *So yes, I believe you.*

The warm electricity is going to leak out my eyes. The relief is so huge I can feel it all the way in those deep, sore spots on my shoulders. *Thank you.*

He smiles.

He goes to his bookshelf, to the clay bowl he made, and gently slips the seeds into it. We look at the bowl of seeds for a minute.

What now? he asks.

Well, I say. *I tried moving my bed away from that spot where I found the apple, to maybe block it or something, but the Fear Maker's still here. Maybe it's more about where he lives? About his house. Maybe by using his house in your painting and my poem . . .*

I think of my notebook and what my grandma said when she gave it to me.

Maybe putting the Fear Maker in poems and art will mean he can't be in the real world as much anymore? I say. *And maybe doing the scary thing the Gardener asked me to do will fix . . . something?* I'm unsure of how well this will work, given all the poems I've already tried to write, but it's worth a shot. Maybe if I can write the right poem . . . maybe entering this contest will give the poem some extra power . . .

Aarush grins and picks up a pen from his desk. *My pen is ready*, he says, holding it out like a lance.

I laugh, grab my pen from my notebook, and cross it over his, like we're two knights getting ready for battle.

Mine too, I say.

I hope.

Seeds: A Poem

Here is the seed of me.
Will you take it, hold it soft?
Plant it in good ground?

If I forget to water yours,
I'm sorry.
Will it hurt

if we plant our seeds too close
together?
Pray for rain

and pass the fertilizer.
I have no clue what this will
grow into

but I hope it's something
the bees will like
with not too many thorns.

Pumpkin Joe's

I sleep in too late on Pumpkin Joe Day. Pumpkin Joe's pops up in the autumn time, an outdoor harvest festival about an hour away from our house, in the weeks leading up to Halloween. Usually Mom or Dad wakes me up so we can get out the door early, but when I come out of my room, they're just waking up, too, groggily stirring milk into their coffee mugs.

Not a great start.

But we make it: Mom, Dad, and me. I slip a few of the sunflower seeds into my pocket from their new mason jar home on my dresser, then climb into the car. Mom turns the key in the ignition, and we're off.

Pumpkin Joe's has:
- The best apple cider in Idaho.
- Face painters and pumpkin carvers.
- Buggy rides through acres of hay, with guitar music playing over the loudspeaker.
- Pumpkin bowling, where Dad once won me a giant plushie potato when he knocked down the most corncob pins.
- Gunnysack slides.
- A goat pen where the goat kids eat right from your hand.

- A giant corn maze we never go in, because I don't understand why you'd want to make yourself feel lost. (I used
  to love it, when I was little. Before the Halloween when I
  was seven. Now it's unsettling even to look at.)

Lots of people here today, Dad says when we pull into the
parking lot. He says it with a resigned sigh.

We wait in line to buy our tickets. *It's more expensive than
last year*, Mom says, while the girl with carefully penciled-in
eyebrows stamps smudgy Pumpkin Joe's logos on our hands.

The girl does not have blank, colorless eyes, so that's good
news.

In fact, in my quick scan after I walk through the front
entry, it seems nobody here is one of the empty-eyed. Unless
you count all the jack-o'-lanterns, of course.

I try my best to take this as a positive sign. A good omen.

So Mom, Dad, and I begin our Pumpkin Joe Day.

We drink apple cider.

We go on the hayride.

None of us talk much.

All three of us feel more anxious and solemn this year than
we did last Pumpkin Joe Day, I think. Is this just how things
are now? What growing up means? Will next year feel more
normal?

We walk down the center of the fair, looking at the different booths. There's a carousel with horses and benches going
up and down, up and down. When it stops, a little girl on a

white horse with black spots painted on its rump cheers and asks her dad to go again again again.

We pass the pumpkin bowling booth, which none of us really feel like doing this year. Past that is a water gun game, and a teenage boy in a backward baseball cap is shooting water into open clown mouths to try to win his girlfriend a neon-green jack-o'-lantern plushie.

We walk through the funhouse mirror tent, and get a soft chuckle when Dad's round belly becomes thin as a pencil in the reflection, squeezing him right in the middle.

There's even a new roller coaster this year with a potato in a cowboy hat on the sign, but it looks like a small one for the really little kids, and I hate roller coasters anyway. Why would I throw my guts around and around like that when they're already being twisted and turned and messed up enough as it is?

I really hate roller coasters.

We get to the big slide, which is probably for little kids, too, but I take a gunnysack and climb to the top while Mom and Dad wait below. I stand quietly in line behind a big group of younger kids and a little girl with sleek black curls who waves and calls down to her mom before she slides.

Maybe today would have been different if Aarush were here. We invited him, but he couldn't come. I think of a story we talked about in school, a story from the ancient Greeks about a former king cursed by the god Hades to forever push and push a giant boulder to the top of a hill, only to have it roll all the way back to the bottom, over and over again. I think of that story because that's a little bit what today feels like—trying to make this trip fun and easy and light like it was before, like it's always been. Trying to push a boulder of happy up a hill of anxiety.

It would probably all be easier, too, if Grandma could come like she used to. But she gets winded and tires quickly if she's on her feet for too long.

I sit on my sack and slip down the slide.

At the bottom, my parents are waiting for me with a plateful of elote, Mexican-style corn on the cob, rolled in mayo, seasoned with lime juice and chili powder, and sprinkled with salty cheese, which they know is my favorite.

Here you go, sweetie, Mom says.

Things are different—heavier—and with Grandma's heart scare and the money stress and everything else going on, I can see it all wearing on them. Mom and Dad are not quite their normal selves. Not as breezy and upbeat as they used to be. It's my Fear Maker out in the world, looming and tall, but I wonder what their Fear Makers would look like. I wish wish wish there was no such thing as Fear Makers, that Pumpkin Joe Day could be as bright and crisp as it's always been, and that Mom and Dad could be as light and easy as they've always seemed to be, but I hold the warm, savory corn, and it means a lot that I can see them trying. I can see them trying really hard.

Things That Don't Work

That night, again, sleep seems like a kickboxing match. At one a.m., I try warm milk. I sneak into the kitchen and use the Monet mug, my favorite. I put the milk in the microwave with cinnamon and a dash of vanilla. I jot down more lines in my notebook, lines for the contest poem I will write with Aarush.

The nightmares still come.

In the school hallway the next day, I hum that song about being afraid, the one from *The King and I*, but when I walk into Mr. Reitman's classroom, his eyes are still colorless, blank, and staring.

Every day I keep seeds in my pocket. Minus the ones I gave to Aarush.

I still hear the Fear Maker's voice from the shadows.

Another night. Another one a.m. I go to the kitchen for a drink.

I stumble down the hallway.

Passing the living room, I glance outside, through the window and into the night.

I swear I see someone looking back.

The silhouette of a tall, thin man with a hint of glowing embers in his eyes.

In that split second I can see the Fear Maker watching me like I'm a trapped fish in a bowl.

But when I blink and look closer, he's gone. Or was he really there at all?

I close the curtains tight and try to remember how to breathe.

The next day, Aarush texts me.

Aarush: ✿??

Me: ☻ nope.

No, I think. No more sunflower garden. Not yet.

But I need it, I think to myself. I thought you were supposed to come when I needed you.

No glow. No Garden.

It's like trying to see all the stars in the sky with a big thick something blocking the view.

But the Gardener said I would find it again, when I needed it the very most. And what else do I have?

Where else in all the wide wide wide wide world can I run to be safe from what's chasing me?

So I'll keep looking.

I'll always keep looking.

Starry Night: Ekphrastic #2

Hello, moon, with your thick halo of glow.
Hello, star spatter, like shining footprints.
Hello, gradated blue hills,
church steeple, house windows
with the lights on.

Me? I am that pale swirl in the sky,
folding around itself.
Even the sky relishes a good view
of chapel bells and starlight.

But you, black tower.
You, black smoke,
or menacing spire,
tree of fear and fire,
blocking the light.
I can't understand
what you're saying
even though the rest of the night
is quiet and you are so loud,
so very, very loud.

Fall

The next week, Mom has an interview for another job, so on Monday after school I go home with Aarush again. Mom hasn't heard back from the first interview yet. I don't know if that's normal or not.

It's weird, Aarush says when we're alone in his room. *My mom brought burgers home for dinner last night. She never gets burgers. I keep asking Dev if he's noticing anything, but he just shrugs and says he likes burgers. I don't think he'd notice if Mom dyed her hair pink as long as she kept giving him food.*

That does seem strange for her, I say.

Yeah, he says. *Very.*

I obviously don't know her as well as you, but did she seem a little more . . . rigid today than normal?

Aarush nods.

He doesn't ask if I believe it's related to the blank eyes, to the Fear Maker, but I'm pretty sure we're both thinking it.

At least we have our plan.

I've been trying to write, I tell him. *The poem for the contest, about the Fear Maker's house. But I just keep crossing out lines. I can't figure out what kind of poem I want it to be.*

Keep trying, Aarush says. *I know you'll figure it out. Maybe we can try going into the woods to write and draw? For inspiration? During the day, of course.*

Maybe, I say, but just that thought makes all my bones feel as stiff and heavy as if someone poured cement into them.

I'm at Aarush's house for only half an hour before Mom calls.

How did it go? is how I answer. The usual doughy, choking block that stifles my words isn't as big in my throat right now. I always feel just a sliver more capable and brave with Aarush.

Grandma's in the hospital, Mom says. Her voice is slightly breathless, serious as drowning.

Hospital. A rolling-boulder word crashing into my gut at full speed. It's like the walls of Aarush's room and everything in it go white, and I wonder if this is what the blank eyes see. If they feel sunk in this fear all the time.

What? I ask. A squeak word.

They said she'll be okay, Mom says. *She passed out and fell and bruised her hip, but they don't think she broke it and they've got her on fluids and are checking her heart. It's going to be okay, Penny. But I'm on my way; I'll be at Aarush's to pick you up in seven minutes. We'll go meet Dad at the hospital.*

I nod, then remember she can't see me, so I whisper, *Okay*, and hang up.

My words are logjammed, stopped up, blocking the top of a Niagara of words and foaming thoughts and every roiling fear.

My grandma, I tell Aarush. *She fell down and she . . . she's not . . .*

We tell Mrs. Banerjee, who makes me a quick peppermint tea.

Aarush sits by me on the front porch. We sip hot drinks and say nothing.

It'll be okay, Aarush says finally, as my mom pulls up.

It'll be okay, says Mom again as we drive.

It'll be okay, says the nurse taking us to Grandma's room.

Dad is in the chair by her bed.

Grandma's eyes are closed, but she opens them when we come in.

Oh, look at all the drama I've caused. I'm fine, she says.

You haven't caused anything, Mom, Dad says. Then he turns to us. *They just finished the EKG.*

Grandma's face is so pale. There's a tube in her arm. The room smells like baby powder and bleach.

She's trying to keep her eyes open, but I see the purple heaviness around them. She has the same tired eyes as the last time we were at the hospital, before she moved into the assisted living home.

What if being tired and sick makes it easier for the Fear Maker to find you? What if Grandma's the next one in the Fear Maker's sights and her trouble is something even worse than an aging heart?

This is all your fault, a voice says. *Did you know, honeybunch, that pennies aren't even worth the cost it takes to make them?*

The Fear Maker's voice out loud again, right behind me, pouring through my eardrums and into my thoughts.

Nobody else responds to the voice. He's talking just to me, and I feel like a vacuum has been turned on inside me and I just want to curl in on myself and disappear. Because what if he's right? What if there was something I could have done? What if, when I let the Fear Maker in, I brought hurt and wreckage to everyone around me?

More beeping. More bustling. Finally, a nurse comes in and tells us Grandma needs her rest.

I'll stay for a while, Dad says.

Let's get home and you can do your homework, Mom says to me. As if I'll be able to focus on homework or anything at all. She puts an arm around me as we walk out through the hospital doors to the parking garage. *Dad will keep us posted. It's going to be okay*, she says again, like she's trying to persuade herself.

Text from Aarush:

Thinking of you, friend. Tell me how Grandma's doing? And how you're doing??

I don't really know what to say.

Every cell in me aches for the Garden, my Garden. Being out here in the heavy world just gets harder and harder.

Chambers

There are four doors in a heart.
Open, close, open, close, for blood
and monsters, open open open
for what Grandma calls the better angels
of our nature—
an open door lets the world in,
vines growing around
the hinges, leaves
carpeting the ventricle floor.
Up there, see the giant heart oak.
In some of these chambers
there are so many roses
so many forget-me-nots and—
coming through that cracked-open door—
so many subtle
deep-rooted
weeds.

Into the Woods

I went into the woods when I was nine.

Right after my birthday.

That birthday, the Fear Maker sent me a nightmare about my parents' heads on silver platters, his own special gift to me.

Go away go away go away. My constant chant.

He didn't listen. He never listens. I woke up after this nightmare feeling mousetrapped, desperate. My parents were ready with a warm quilt, my grandma ready with her soothing tide of words.

But it wasn't working. It wasn't making the Fear Maker go away. I was nine, and it was June, and I was forced to take drastic measures. As drastic as trying to confront the Fear Maker in person. In the woods. Maybe then he'd take me seriously.

I put on my tennis shoes and my favorite yellow socks. I put on my jeans with the sparkly buttons. When I told my mom I was going exploring, she hesitated for a second. On one page of her face I read surprise—I hadn't wanted to go out on my own in a long, long time. On the other page I read a line or two of relief, and the thought that maybe, just maybe, my asking to do something a little brave meant that things were getting better. That I was getting better.

I couldn't tell her it was the opposite.

Okay, she said. *But as soon as the sun starts setting, you need to be back here.*

I told her I'd be back long before that. No way was I going to be out there in the dark.

A quick peanut butter and honey sandwich for lunch, then I stepped out into our backyard, the screen door clapping shut behind me. I felt like Gretel going into the witch's lair without Hansel, and I convinced myself that the trick was to not think too hard about it, but to jump in before I could chicken out. So I hurried down our back steps and across the lawn and through the gate to where the trees began.

I followed what I'd seen in my nightmares. I startled a bushy-tailed little squirrel that scolded me as I hurried past. I kept careful bearings so I could find my way home again, but I walked fast. Just get this over with, I thought.

The thicker and creepier the woods got, the more familiar they seemed. I'd seen the path to the Fear Maker's house many times in my nightmares, and I knew I was getting close. I squeezed between trees growing closer and closer together. I barreled on, trying to ignore the warning siren thoughts getting louder and louder in my head. I stopped only to dislodge a twig that got tangled in my shoelaces.

And then I was there.

I'd followed the route from my nightmares and the trees opened up into a small clearing, and in the middle of that clearing was a house.

The Fear Maker's house was smaller then, when I was nine. The steps up to the porch weren't finished. There was no rocking chair or shutters, only boarded-up spaces where the windows would be. There was a little bit of scaffolding around the back, making space for more rooms. The whole thing seemed slightly tilted, like a corpse rising up from a grave.

A corpse, yes, but one that was living and growing. Maybe instead it was a seed, like the seed of a poison apple tree, getting bigger and sturdier every day, growing into something malevolent but not yet awake.

I stood there for a long time, staring. Those warning sirens were catching up with me fast, and my breath was coming only in short gasps. Even the grass in the clearing seemed wrong, somehow, and it took me a moment to figure out what it was. The grass seemed to be growing from the ground like normal, but the color was an unnatural monochrome. A single shade of not-quite-right green. A real artist would know that there are a dozen shades of green in a single blade of grass, hints of browns and several yellows, too.

But I knew what I'd come there to do. If the Fear Maker wasn't going to listen to me when I told him to leave, all I had left was to demand it face-to-face.

I took a few shaky steps into the clearing, feeling utterly alone and so, so small, like a lamb stepping up to a pack of wolves. My throat was dry and scratchy and my words had tumbled out of me somewhere back in the trees, so I was a lamb who couldn't even bleat.

I stood, frozen, anxious for my mouth to work again so I could say what I'd come to say, even if I said it badly.

Then the door clicked and cracked open. Just a little bit, a half-awake creature half opening one eye.

And from somewhere deep inside, in the shadowy rooms of that house, I heard laughing.

The same laughter that rang in my ears when I woke up mid-panic with streaming eyes and a damp, sweat-soaked T-shirt. The same laughter that echoed in my nightmares as I tried to save my parents and failed again and again and again.

Laughter from someone who I knew now would never listen to me, no matter what I said. Whose only goal in their whole existence was to eat me alive.

I turned and ran.

I ran out of the clearing, the laughter rumbling behind me. I followed the path back home, thinking only about getting away from that clearing as fast as I could. I kicked up dirt and twigs behind me and stirred up a noisy cohort of crows.

Home. I ran up the back steps and yanked open the screen door so hard that for a second I was worried I'd damaged the hinges. Mom was in the kitchen and she didn't falter when I barreled into her; she just wrapped her arms around me and stood still while the warmth of her and the smell of baking orange rolls calmed my clattering nerves.

Shh, shh, she said, while my shaking settled down and my dirty, wet face smudged up her apron. She pulled a shriveled leaf from my hair. *Shh, it's okay. It's okay.*

After that day, I heard Mom and Dad whispering more and more about what was happening in my head, how maybe they needed to find someone who could help. After that day, I got better and better at keeping the nightmares to myself, so they wouldn't have to worry about them, too, until those whispers about me and my scared brain started fading again.

But for that minute in the kitchen, I was glad to hear her say it was okay. Even though I knew it wasn't. Even though the nightmares didn't—haven't—gone away.

Even though, now, the wolf's coming out of the woods.

Dad Comes Home Late

I hear the creak of the front door and his heavy steps. I haven't fallen asleep yet for lots of reasons, and I get out of bed and head to the kitchen with the excuse of needing a drink.

He's sitting at the table, looking into his own glass.

Hi, sweetie, he says.

How is she? I ask.

Okay. Tired. Sore. But she's gonna be okay.

Good, I say. But will she, really? With the Fear Maker out there, will anyone?

I get a glass from the cabinet and there's a quiet splashing sound while I fill it up at the fridge. Dad's staring into space. There's something different about his face, like worry has etched new edges there. Normally his face is round, soft, the kind that makes people nod when they hear he works in a flower shop.

Wilted. That's how he looks now.

Not like his usual self.

My glass leaves a little ring of wet on the wood table.

Dad, I say. *What's your favorite flower today?*

He keeps staring. One second. Three seconds.

Huh? Oh. Oh, I'm sorry, sweetie, I can't even think. Ask me tomorrow.

So I go to bed and find shadows of open, hungry mouths in the walls and wonder how late Dad will stay up and how fast the Fear Maker is coming.

The House

It's a malignant, wooden, shuttered, watching house.

It's the house Aarush drew. There in front of me. A house I saw years ago, but it's grown bigger now. It isn't sleeping anymore.

Everything's quiet while I stand there looking at the house, the rickety front steps that are finished now, the heavy front door. There are thick trees all around, trees with reaching limbs and gripping fingers.

I've seen so many different things every time I've nightmared into that house, but this time I know I'm going to find the Fear Maker himself. In the dream, I'm walking up those steps, up to the door, and I can't stop myself. I know I'm going in and will never come back out.

I hear a hard, cold laugh.

That's the dream.

That's the nightmare.

I wake up.

I turn on my lamp and reach for my notebook. Cold sweat and shaking hands again.

I will capture this house with my pen. I have to. There's a jumble of jotted lines from all my previous nightmares, but I will find a way to bring it all together. I will try again and again.

The paper flutters as I flip to the end. To an empty page.

But the page I land on isn't empty. And it isn't my writing.

There are just two words, written in familiar script and in a deep red ink.

Hello, Penny.

My eyes stream in fury and I pound the mattress under me. I rip out the page and tear it into tiny confetti pieces.

You can't do this to me. You can't.

I flip to a fresh page and click my pen ready. But the words don't come. I scratch out line after line, trying again to get this right and failing failing failing.

My Monster's House

My monster's house is full of rot

My monster's house cannot be forgot

My monster's house is a mouth with teeth

My monster's house has graves underneath

~~My monster's house will eat me alive~~

~~My monster's house ????~~

Equations

Only a couple of days before Halloween, and Mr. Reitman isn't laughing anymore. His face is stiff, neutral, and the colorless eyes stare ahead, stare at the board like they see nothing. Face like a mask. Voice even and mechanical, as if his voice box is being played like an instrument, like all of what makes him *him* is gone. Including the mean, grumpy stuff. And that's how he stands up there and teaches us about points, lines, and angles.

I think of what the Gardener told me about empty shells, moving through empty motions.

Mr. Reitman's still acting weird, isn't he? I whisper to Mismatched Socks Girl after the bell rings. (Her name is Carmen—I found out when she dropped her notebook last week and I saw her name when I picked it up for her. Although today her socks actually match, for once. Both black-and-white striped.)

She says, *Yeah*, and shrugs.

Still nobody sees the nothing-eyes, but at least they're noticing something's off.

Mom and Dad are both waiting in the car after school. They're not talking, and no music is on. With Dad in the car he'd normally be playing something opera-y like Pavarotti.

The silence presses down like a weighted blanket as we drive to the hospital.

Mom doesn't ask me about school. Dad angry-mutters at the blue Corolla ahead of him that's going too slow.

This isn't like them. Not like them at all.

Grandma is sitting up in bed when we see her. A tray of mostly eaten toast and applesauce is on the side table. There's a tiny bit of color back in her cheeks, and she smiles when she sees me.

There's my lucky Penny. Come here, my girl.

She wraps me in a soft, secure hug.

Someone, at least, is getting a little bit back to normal. I hope this—seeing Grandma okay—will help my parents be less anxious, be a little bit back to normal, too, but some part of me is certain that something much worse is going on.

No, I don't want to even think about that.

How are you feeling? I ask Grandma.

Much better.

I sit on the edge of the bed and she runs a hand over my hair. *You?* she asks. *You look worried about something.*

You mean besides you? I say, trying to seem casual. But Grandma puts her hand softly over mine. She's not going to let me off that easily.

I glance at my parents. They're checking something on Mom's phone. I look down at my hands. *Yeah,* I admit.

In stiff voices Mom and Dad ask Grandma if she's okay, if the doctors and nurses are taking good care of her. The chat stops after a minute or two. Dad says he's going to get us snacks from the vending machine. Mom's phone buzzes. *I'm sorry,* she says. *I have to take this; it might be that interview.*

Then it's just me and Grandma in the hospital room with the beeping machine and the mechanical bed and the cupboards full of tubes and vomit trays.

What are you worried about, honey? Grandma says.

My tongue won't loosen with the words, like it's a Fruit Roll-Up rolled up tight. I'm too full up with worry and the ripe smell of hospital soap.

Grandma nods, understanding, like a doctor diagnosing a problem.

How's the poetry coming? she asks.

That loosens, a touch, my squeaky-hinge mouth.

I miss you reading poems to me at night, I say.

Grandma pats my hand. *I miss that, too*, she says. *But those poems will always be there when you need them, even if I'm farther away than before.*

Just like what the Gardener said about the Garden, I think. It's like his words and that Garden sun are a mug of cocoa warming me from the inside, and Grandma's poems and hugs are the security blanket wrapping me up safe on the outside.

I'm going to enter a poetry contest with Aarush, I say. *But what I've been trying hasn't really been working.* I don't tell her the reason it's not working is because it has to be the perfect monster-banishing poem. And nothing I write is ever that perfect.

A contest with Aarush? That's wonderful! He's a good egg. And I know how slow the poems come sometimes, believe me. What kinds have you been trying? Free verse? Haiku? I know I had a book of poetic forms at one point...

I've tried a few short forms like haiku, I say. *But they're hard. They seem like . . . a lot. What about you? What's your favorite kind?*

Grandma leans back in the bed. While I can tell she's definitely looking better, I can also tell that talking is tiring her out. But she smiles and says, *Oh, I'm a fan of a good old-fashioned sonnet. They just strike me as so strong and robust, like they can take on anything. At first they seem intimidating, but remember, you're the one holding the pen. Sonnets can do a lot, but once you've got into the flow, they can actually be quite straightforward.*

A sonnet. Strong and robust, hmm? Then maybe that's the best kind of poem for putting nightmares away away away.

She thinks for a moment, still smiling. *Have I read you any of Shakespeare's sonnets? Don't let the bard intimidate you. He's actually quite hilarious. Look up Sonnet 130. It makes me chuckle just thinking about it.*

I don't know about sonnets being straightforward, I think to myself, but maybe I'll try one. I'll look up that Sonnet 130 and use it as a spark for my own poem. For the contest. For Grandma.

You know, Grandma says. *I've always wondered if a sad limerick could be possible. Or a scary one.* She winks at me. *No doubt you could write it, lucky Penny.*

Limerick

The Fear Maker's smile is wide.
He beckons and calls you inside.
A voice in your ear
says, It's too late, my dear.
You're mine and there's nowhere to hide.

Text from Aarush

Aarush: Yeah, it's official. My parents have been acting weird. Not themselves, something's off. Yours?

There's a picture, too. It's a picture of Aarush's gentle, kind mom, but in this photo her face is stiff. She's in the front room of their house, staring, her head turned toward the camera, her mouth a hard straight line.

Her eyes a blank, blank nothing.

Aarush can tell something is wrong, because it's his mom, even though he can't see those blank eyes. What am I supposed to say to him?

I'm in my room and I pace back and forth, back and forth, wearing the carpet thin. I lock my door. I put my hand on my little mason jar of sunflower seeds, wondering about the Gardener, where he is, if he knows what's going on.

This is my fault. If I hadn't given the Fear Maker that candy, that latch-point into the tangible world, none of this would have happened. This is my Fear Maker doing all the damage. What if . . . what if the Banerjees meeting me is what put them in danger? What if Aarush thinks that, too?

What if I haven't found the Gardener again because he's

decided I really am to blame for this mess, and he can't help someone as bad as me?

Me: I am so sorry, Aarush.

It's too hard to tell him they're gone. It's too hard to say, the Fear Maker got them. But Aarush understands.

Aarush: What do we do now?

What do we do now?
What do we do now?

My Monster Sonnet

My monster's eyes glow red like a blood moon
My monster's thoughts march into my brain
~~Up the stairs, the footsteps come soon~~
aslkdjfaklsghdalkhakls

None of this would have happened if it wasn't for me.

The House Swallows Me Whole

And I wake up feeling eaten alive. My body and blood constrict, like I'm sliding down a boa constrictor's esophagus. It's four a.m., the nothing-time. Is this what the Fear Maker does? Is this what the devoured souls feel as they're stolen? Maybe this is what it is to have your soul swallowed and used as fertilizer for the Fear Maker's growing, twisting house. But the remaining bodies? I don't think they feel anything at all.

That house again. The chilled night sweats and clammy palms again.

Like I'm still in the nightmare, I can feel the open door of the house rushing toward me, hungry. It's even bigger than before, growing with the addition of each devoured soul.

I turn on my lamp and try to take deep breaths, pulling in air to the bottom of my lungs, but it's not really working.

The corner of a note pokes out from under my pillow.

I don't need to guess who it's from.

It's the same note from before, the note from my notebook, on the same paper. I can see the jagged lines where I ripped the note to shreds, but the paper is back together again, the torn paper scarred, but those two words whole and crooked.

Hello, Penny.

And there's more, this time.

This time, when I unfold the paper, there in the center is a single human tooth.

A tooth stolen from one of his blank-eyed victims.

I drop the paper and its gruesome contents. I feel so trapped and exposed. I want to sob and scream and rage all at once. I'm shaking so hard my muscles are difficult to control. Stumbling, I manage to reach the bathroom and flick on the light. I still want to check my eyes, my face, just to be sure. My eyes are wide with shock, heavy with exhaustion, but they are still, at least for now, mine. My face is as gray as a blizzard, but it is my face. I get a handful of toilet paper, nauseously pick up the tooth from my bedroom floor, and flush it down the toilet.

What if the Gardener really has given up on me?

That thought tumbles down on me like an Everest-sized avalanche.

An avalanche that will bury me because I'm just too weak to climb out.

And maybe, in the end, even the Gardener knows I'm just too gutless.

I can't be inside anymore. I can't get away from that feeling of a grip on my ankle, red eyes staring at me through the window. In every blink I see that house in the trees opening wide toward me: its meal.

I need the air and sky.

Careful not to wake Mom and Dad, I hurry downstairs and out the front door. The wind on the porch is brisk and biting, which feels exactly right. My eyes water in the chill and my skin prickles awake.

The streetlamps down the street are all on. The windows across the street are dark, and I wonder if anyone is awake in there, and what they'd be able to see if they looked out their window in my direction. Would they see me standing here, or would it be too dark?

Then the cold hits me in a new way. Suddenly, I'm entirely alone, just me, eleven years old, outside on an October night in north Idaho without a sweater. I'm alone in twelve-degree winds, monsters I've released running amok, nightmares ready to eat me alive, and there's no moon to see by.

It's time, I tell myself. I don't care that my parents have been acting so strange, so not themselves. They're still my parents, and I need them. Right now. It's time to talk.

But before I turn around, the light changes. This light is warm, both in color and feel, and my skin stops its prickling.

When I turn around, my front door is glowing a soft, welcoming yellow.

What I Know

I don't have to look for him. The Gardener is there, waiting for me, when I step through, and I collapse into his open arms. I'm sure I'm snotting up his soft brown shirt, but his arms pull tight around me like he'll hold me up as long as I need, as long as the tears are streaming and my legs are wobbling.

"I know what you said, but this is my fault. It's all my fault." It comes out in chokes.

The Gardener keeps his arms strong around my trembling shoulders. For a long time he doesn't say anything. There's a breeze in the sunflowers around us, like the flowers themselves are cooing *hush hush hush*.

He steps back, a hand on my shoulder, his blue eyes as steady as an ocean looking back at me. "Are you listening, Penny?" he says. "This isn't your fault. This is his fault. He's the one who took advantage of your kindness and good heart. He's the one who's stealing souls. What matters is where you go from here. What matters is—do you hear me, Penny?— What matters is that you have the power to defeat him."

"I don't know," I say. My wet face is dripping. His eyes have so much faith in them, they're almost too bright to look at. "I don't know if I do."

"Listen to me," he says. "He destroys and distorts, but he can't build and create like you can. Only you have that power."

Then a short, sobbing laugh bursts out of me. "You sound like my grandma's poems."

The Gardener grins and one of his rough, earthy thumbs wipes my cheek. "Well, we know where you get your wisdom and talent." He tucks clammy strands of hair behind my ears, both his hands resting softly for a moment on my head. "Penelope Hope," he says. "I'm always right here. I'm not going anywhere."

Maybe it's the flowers, blazingly rich as if Van Gogh himself created them, or maybe it's the Gardener's comforting voice and summer-ocean eyes, but I breathe again, a little easier. I have the power to defeat the Fear Maker? I don't know if I believe it, but I believe the Gardener believes it—believes in me—and that means something. That does matter.

We walk around the corner, through the sunflowers that reach above both our heads. A ladybug lands on my pinkie finger, stays a moment, then flies off. I smell the rich soil and the spice of sunflowers.

"That house in the woods. The one I tried to . . . tried to go into, before. I see it growing in my nightmares. I see a locked door. A door at the center of his house. All the souls he's eaten are in there, aren't they?"

The Gardener nods.

"But if that's how he's building his house since I saw it last time . . . if those souls are what he feeds his house with, how can I possibly save them?"

The Gardener's voice is gravelly and gruff, but so soft and gentle. "I wish I could tell you," he says. "It's different for each

Fear Maker, for each person, what they keep at the center. But I can tell you what to bring. And when you get there, you'll know."

I nod. I feel at the same time as if I'm putting on strong armor and as if I'm stepping blindfolded off a cliff.

Ahead is our mint-green bench. The Gardener motions to it.

"How are you feeling?" he says. We both sit.

"I'm okay," I say.

There's a deep trench across his brow, his face full of tenderness and worry. He clears his throat.

"It's time, isn't it?" I say before he can speak. Because I can feel the truth of it myself. As if everything's been building to this moment, everything since the Fear Maker came that Halloween years ago. Some part of me has always known it would come to this, but that's something I've been trying not to know, even if I felt it that day when I walked into the woods and found the Fear Maker's house. Something that poems and sunflowers have made me just brave enough to see.

"The rearranging, the poetry contest—those are just bandages," I say. "They won't fix the problem."

A single cloud floats breezily across the sun.

"I have to go back to his house in the woods and fight him face-to-face."

The Gardener nods.

"But what about the other thing, the scary thing I was supposed to do? What if I'm not ready? I haven't sent a poem to the contest yet. I haven't done the scary thing."

"Haven't you?"

I think back. Maybe the hard thing isn't what I thought. No, I haven't submitted a poem to be judged, but I told Aarush my story. Trusted him with it. That was scary. I looked Mr. Reitman in his colorless blank eyes and didn't run. That was scary, too.

Those scary things—I did them, and I'm still alive. Still breathing.

The Gardener takes off his straw hat and lets the sun filter through his scruffy, wiry hair.

"Are you him?" I say. "Are you Van Gogh?" It's not what I was planning to say.

He smiles.

"Is that who I look like here?" the Gardener says. "Oh, that's just fine with me. He's one of my favorites. A good man." He looks down at his hands, his smile fading like that cloud passing across the sun. "His Fear Maker was one I won't ever forget."

So we sit on the bench, the Gardener and I. I remember asking him the first time we met how he knew so much about the Fear Maker, and those shadow-scars make even more sense, now. But so do the sunflowers.

I sit on my hands, the metal perfectly warm beneath my palms. Again I feel like someone who can say yes to things here in this Garden, though I don't know if that will last after I walk out through the doors, back to the real world. Real world? No, no, that's not right. If anything, this Garden is what's Real, and everything else is shadow.

A beat of silence. I know what I have to ask. "What do I need to do?"

Heart

One of my grandma's poems has a line that says, *No limestone expects the strength of raindrops.* I think of that line while the Gardener tells me what I need to do. I think of that line while I imagine a house in the deepest part of the woods, a maze house, a trap house, that will consume anyone who dares believe they can venture in and free the devoured souls.

Anyone, in other words, like me.

Here is what the Gardener tells me:

Get to the heart of the house, free the souls, destroy the Fear Maker.

That's what matters.

We are sitting on our bench, watching a sparrow.

"How do I do it?" I say. "Once I'm at the heart of the house, how do I destroy the Fear Maker?"

"I don't know." The Gardener shakes his head. "I wish I did. This is your Fear Maker. But when you reach the center, you will know."

I keep my eyes on the closest sunflower, looking at each petal, each ridged seed at the flower's core. The flower's vibrancy is keeping me going like a transfusion of life and color, and I doubt my ability to keep upright without it.

"What if I don't? What if I can't, if I'm too scared? What if I fail?"

"Then I'll be right here," says the Gardener. His voice is as firm as the ground under our feet.

As if emphasizing his words, the Gardener reaches into his coat pockets and pulls out two big palmfuls of sunflower seeds, which he pours into my cupped hands. I hold on to those seeds tight, like they're my harness as I rappel off the side of a cliff.

"Okay," I say. "Okay, I'll do it. I'll try. But you might have to point me in the right direction."

What If Little Red

What if Little Red was wrong
when she thought fresh bread and a red hood
could make her brave?

What if the basket of goodies
started out light and got
heavier and heavier?

What if she had to start down the path
knowing the danger, knowing she and Grandma
might lose?

What if it was always harder
to see the sun
through the trees?

What if she already knew
about the Big Bad Wolf
and what he'd done?

What if Little Red knew exactly
why the person she was walking toward
had such big teeth?

Better and Worse Worse Worse

I sleep a little, back in my own room. Now it's the day before Halloween here in the real world—the un-Garden—and it takes me longer than usual to get ready for school. *Hurry*, says Mom. *What's the deal?* says Dad. But it's like my muscles know what I'm gearing up to do and they're refusing to cooperate, like all my movements are pushing through Jell-O.

I want to say, *Help me.* I want to say, *Please tell me how to fight a monster like this one.*

Instead, I say, *Can we make orange rolls tonight?*

Mom says, *Not tonight, honey.*

What about painting pillowcases? I have some ideas.

Another time. I'm sorry, sweetie.

It's so easy to listen to that tension in my muscles—my body saying *nope nope nope* as I walk the school hallways. I start thinking of all the things I'd rather do than go into the woods to the Fear Maker's house, like sleeping on the school roof or cleaning the urinals in the boys' bathroom.

During lunch I get a text from Aarush.

Aarush: ✿??

Me: Yes. He told me what to bring to fight the Fear Maker.

Aarush: WHAT????? Call me ASAP! We need to discuss! Plan!

Aarush: Can we save my parents?

I don't know how to respond. I eat the peanut butter and honey sandwich my mom packed for me, but I don't really taste it.

After Aarush's text, I imagine what's happening to his parents happening to mine, and I imagine my grandma's heart getting even worse, and I think that there are in fact a few things that would be worse than knocking on the Fear Maker's door.

In Mr. Reitman's class I take out my homework, my pencils, and set them on my desk. Lift your head up, I tell myself, but everything is so heavy. I arrange my pencils, grip the edges of my chair, and look up at Carmen, her back toward me.

Just acknowledgment, I think. A friendly face, that's all I need right now. I reach out and tap Carmen's shoulder. Maybe my excuse can be asking for a pencil sharpener, or if she was confused on question eight like I was. Anything.

When she turns around and faces me, her eyes are blank, colorless, and wide.

This Time

This time I clutch my seeds and barely make it until the final bell.

This time I'm at home and my lungs still won't inhale properly.

This time I'm not sleeping.

This time I pace back and forth in my bedroom, my feet running electricity from the carpet up to my hair.

This time I can hear the TV static from the family room, like it's been left on the wrong channel.

This time I can feel the woods, the nightmares, all closing in, and I know it's time for me to talk.

I think of the blank-eyed people, more and more of them. I know my parents have mountains on their shoulders, but I have to tell them what's been going on. It's past time. With the baker, with Mr. Reitman, now with Carmen . . . I don't think I can carry this on my own anymore. I don't know how to make it all stop.

This time I breathe in deep, open my door, and head downstairs.

This time my parents are on the couch
watching nothing on TV
and their eyes are blank caverns—white, wide emptiness.
I feel alone in a world of that boundless, blank emptiness.

Like my screams would only turn to echoes. I wait for the nightmare to end.

This time I don't wake up.

This time the nightmare is real.

Can't Do It

Can't do it Can't do it Can't do it Can't do it Can't do it
Can't do it Can't do it Can't do it Can't do it Can't do it Can't
do it Can't do it Can't do it Can't do it Can't do it Can't do it
Can't do it Can't do it Can't do it I'm just one person What do
I do Can't do it Can't do it Can't do it Can't do it Can't Can't
Can't

Me?

No one here but fear and

Everything changing, everyone gone but

Night comes quick and grows inside

Who else is alone as

Mom, Dad, can you see

Do you still love

A world of shadows and rot and

Who do they think can possibly fight
    the Fear Maker?

Penny in the World

Behind the shut door of my closet I try to pull enough oxygen into my lungs, but it's not working. I bury my face in the purple sweater hanging above me, the one I got for Christmas last year. I thought there might be less world entering into my brain if I was in my small, harmless closet, but that's not working, either. So I try the reverse tactic, and imagine myself as a red pin on Google Maps, thinking about exactly where I am. It runs through my head like a chant—Penny in her closet in her bedroom in her house in Coeur d'Alene in Idaho in the United States in North America in the World.

It doesn't help, either.

What if the Fear Maker's goal is to take away everyone I know, steal each soul one by one, until I'm the only one left? So that I'm absolutely, completely alone when he finally comes to take me? It keeps happening faster and faster. I thought I'd have more time before I had to go deep into the woods to the Fear Maker's house.

There's one person who might know what to do. And she hasn't been taken—yet.

Hunched under sweatshirts and pants legs draping down over me from their hangers, I call my grandma.

She only came home from the hospital that day, while I was at school, and I worry she'll still be resting, away from her phone.

She answers after one ring.

I tell her everything.

There's a Fear Maker, and I let him loose.

I see the people whose souls he's devoured—their glassy, white, blank eyes.

He's getting closer and closer. He's reaching out from under my bed and leaving rotten teeth under my pillow. He took people at the bakery, a girl at school, Aarush's parents, my teacher.

Now he's taken Mom and Dad.

And it's up to me to find them. To face the Fear Maker and bring them back. Before he can take anyone else—her, or Aarush, or me.

Grandma listens carefully and doesn't answer for a long time. I hear her steady breaths and imagine her considering. I put my hand in the light coming from under my closet door.

She might just tell me to go to bed. She might be thinking I'm back to the kinds of nightmares I used to have when I was seven and eight, although those feel like tame little kittens compared with the rabid lion I'm facing now. She might be thinking the thing I'm thinking—

I don't think I can do it, I say.

Grandma takes a deep breath. *Why's that?* she says.

The question takes me a bit off guard. I thought it seemed so obvious. *Because . . . because he's the Fear Maker. If he's taken so many other people, even grown-ups—if he can take Mom and Dad, how am I supposed to do any better? I'm only one girl. I'm just me.*

Exactly, Grandma says. *And how do you know that's not just what's needed to beat this monster? What if you're his kryptonite? What if you're actually more powerful than he is? Ten times more powerful?*

I hug my knees and my pinkie finds a new hole in my jeans. I keep thinking of those eyes and the watching trees and the sinister Fear Maker notes I find in places that should be safe.

But something about Grandma's voice makes me think of sunflowers, too. I remember what Grandma said about monsters, and it almost doesn't matter if she believes in the Fear Maker or not. She believes in the fight. And I remember what the Gardener said, that the Fear Maker twists and distorts, but doesn't create things like I do. That I have everything I need to defeat the Fear Maker in me already.

I don't know, I say. Which I suppose is better than *I can't*.

I do, Grandma says. *Maybe you have power he can't even imagine.*

Halloween

When I open my eyes again, it's Halloween.

I stand behind my locked bedroom door, listening to see if the soulless husks of my parents are on the other side. Everything seems quiet.

I start by calling Aarush. I tell him about my mom and dad.

Tonight, we agree. *Before anyone else gets stolen.* It's time to fight the Fear Maker. It's time to save our parents before it's too late. Trick-or-treating gives us the perfect excuse, and no one will see us go into the woods in the dark.

Okay, what do we know already? Aarush says. *What do we know about that house? What do you remember?*

I think back to my years-ago trek into the woods. The thought of going back makes me want to puke, but I'm also a little more prepared this time. I have Grandma's words and the Gardener's sunflower seeds, and I have Aarush. But even still, returning to that house—this time knowing I have to go inside—well, I've never done anything harder.

I feel that Fear Maker seed inside me pulling. Pulling like a string, like a monstrous, tethering umbilical cord, if I'm brave enough to follow where it leads.

I'll be able to find the house, I say.

Okay, Aarush says. *Okay.* He sounds like he's gearing himself up, too.

Even back then, when the house was . . . younger, it made me feel like it was just waiting to eat me, I say. *And now it's bigger. It's like it's woken up. If my nightmares are correct.*

That makes sense, Aarush says. *Everything about the Fear Maker seems like it's getting bigger, and that's how come he's now reaching out of the woods.*

Yeah, I say. *Exactly. Now, in my nightmares, it looks just like that house you drew. The rocking chair, rickety stairs, everything.*

You remember a lot of your nightmares, Aarush says.

They're not normal nightmares, I say.

I think back to what I've seen in my dreams over the years. Even though the outside of the house has grown, it's still the same structure I saw when I was nine. The inside of the house . . . that's trickier.

When I'm dreaming, I say, *what I find when I go inside the house always changes. Almost like it's alive in there. The rooms shift, like a maze with changing walls, so maps or anything like that won't do us any good. It's like every room is a new trap I've never seen before. And then at the center is the locked door. Behind that door is the heart of the house, where he keeps the souls he's taken.*

Okay, Aarush says. *Okay, we can still do this. The Gardener told you to bring sunflower seeds and your poetry notebook, correct?*

Yes.

Then that must be what we need to get through the traps.

Yes, I say. *Right.* I don't know how sunflower seeds and my scrawled poems will help us survive the Fear Maker's house, but if the Gardener says that's what to bring, that's what I'll bring.

I want to take my grandma's book, too, I say.

Good idea, says Aarush. *And I'll bring water bottles and snacks.*

After I hang up, I put on my favorite green T-shirt and jeans with the gold thread daisies embroidered on the pockets. (Dad says daisies are the happiest flowers.) A lot of kids will be wearing their costumes at school today, but for now, I want safe. I want familiar.

Before I unlock my door and leave my room, I carefully put a handful of seeds into my pocket.

Like walking through a minefield, I open my door and tiptoe into the hallway. I step lightly down the stairs and hear one clink from the kitchen. I peek around the doorway.

Mom and Dad are there, eyes white and blank as empty cups.

Mom sits at the table, staring at nothing, her hand on her coffee mug. Dad stands by the counter, and when the coffee maker beeps, he pours coffee into his mug, his arm as stiff as a lever on a factory conveyor belt. Every morning I watch him pour cream and scoop too much sugar into his coffee, but not today. Eyes wide, he sips from his mug as if he can't taste it at all.

I take a deep breath. I think about what Grandma said, that I could be more powerful than the Fear Maker. I think about my and Aarush's plan. I put my hand on the seeds in my pocket.

I hurry into the kitchen, dashing toward the bananas by the fridge.

Good morning, says Dad, stiff.

Good morning, says Mom, like a reflex.

Neither of them looks at me.

I snatch a banana and head back out toward the front door. *I'll take the bus today*, I say.

Neither of them says they know how much I hate the bus.

Neither of them asks why I'm not wearing my costume.

They don't say anything at all.

I'm coming to save you, I think, wanting to beam my thoughts at their souls, their real selves, in that room deep in the Fear Maker's house. I don't know if I'll make it, but I'm coming.

As I walk out the front door, I feel the blank white eyes of whatever is left of my parents staring at the nape of my neck.

Halloween: A Poem

Mummies unravel,
revealing their rot.
A real witches' brew
bubbles up in its pot.

Put on a costume or cape
if you dare.
You won't see the masks
that the real monsters wear.

You have no real powers,
despite your red cape,
so what door will you knock on
before it's too late?

This Halloween, monsters
are stalking the streets.
The tricks are all haunting,
and the treats

are rotten and poisoned and deadly indeed.

Tap Tap Tap

A branch from a bone-bare tree knocks on the classroom window all through math. Mr. Reitman doesn't notice. He just goes on talking in a droning, inhuman voice about radius and area. His white, blank eyes take in nothing. I try not to flinch at each little tree jab, and wonder if Mr. Reitman's real self can see my parents' real selves in that place where they're all trapped.

I'll try to help you, too, I think, as he writes on the board.

Since Mr. Reitman's back is turned (and he's not really here, anyway), I check my phone under my desk. Two texts from Aarush:

Aarush: Bag packed, complete with Oreos and flashlights. I'll meet you at that 7-Eleven on the corner at 7:30.

Aarush: I really want my parents back.

I think about what we're going to do tonight. I have never been more terrified.

But I've also never felt more certain. Not confident, necessarily, but certain. My hands are cold but steady. Because I have to do this. *Have* to. In a lot of ways, this is about saving myself—saving my body from becoming an empty shell, saving my dreams from turning entirely to nightmare—as well as rescuing my parents and Aarush's parents and all the other people trapped somewhere deep in the heart of the Fear Maker's haunted house. I hold the sunflower seeds tight in my palm. Each one is a breath of clean air from the Garden. Each one is a memory of the Gardener looking me in the eyes and saying, *You are brave. You are strong. You are good.* It's like those words are planted in me, growing bright and strong.

He is my strength on the inside. Grandma, my strength on the outside. And my best friend, the strength by my side.

I text Aarush back.

Me: I'll be there.

Me: And me too.

Things You Can't Buy at 7-Eleven

At the 7-Eleven on the corner
where Mom used to take you
to get Diet Coke and Blue Raspberry Slushies
(when she was really your mom)
there are some things you can't buy.

You can't buy courage
in a little fun-sized plastic wrapper
with a caramel toffee center.

The clerk behind the counter
is a kid just a few years older than you
with a chicken pox scar on his left eyebrow,

not a wizard behind the curtain
who can sell you a stout heart,
or a monster-fighting brain.

You? All you have is this pen,
a pocket full of seeds,
and a friend walking toward you

under the streetlight.

Ready, Set

Aarush is in a black hoodie and I'm in my green one. His face looks grim but firm and determined. I hope mine does, too.

Hi, he says.

Hi, I say.

Under this streetlamp, we're on an island of light, about to step off into very murky waters. There are a few kids on the other side of the street, a little younger than us, in dinosaur and princess and zombie costumes.

I turn to Aarush and square my shoulders.

Ready? I say.

Not yet, he says, sliding his backpack off his shoulders. *We may as well go in as prepared as possible.* He unzips his bag and pulls out a package of Oreos, two protein bars, and two filled-up water bottles. My guts feel jittery, but I swallow the food down. No sense going into battle on an empty stomach. The Fear Maker's house won't be empty, that's for sure. We stand there quietly and eat the bars and a handful of Oreos each. Beyond the light, at the end of the street, I can see the corner of my house and the thick woods behind it.

Drink at least a third of this, Aarush says, handing me a water bottle with sunflowers on it. *We may as well go in hydrated.*

I don't know whether to laugh or scream.

I drink the water.

This is the weirdest picnic ever, I say.

After we're done, Aarush puts what's left back in his back-pack, swapping the cookies out for two flashlights. He hands me one.

I have extra batteries, too, he says.

I'm really, really glad you're here, I say.

He just nods.

He shoulders his backpack.

I put my hand on my pocket, patting my sunflower seeds.

We face the night, flashlights in hand.

Ready? I say.

Set, he says.

We step forward.

The Things We Carry

When Aarush and I pass my house, I don't look back. My parents aren't there anyway. Not really. They're somewhere in the heart of the twisted woods ahead of me. Trapped in a house surrounded by this army of bare branches and sticky, spiky pine.

You really know where you're going? Aarush asks as we step through the tree line.

Unfortunately, yes, I say. I remember the path to the Fear Maker's house like I'd walked it just yesterday, and I've seen this path in my nightmares many, many times before. But it's more than just that. With each step I can feel that tug in my stomach pulling me forward, like that apple seed was bait on a hook and I'm now being reeled slowly, slowly in.

The night sky makes every step eerier than the last. The landmarks from before, and from my nightmares, are all there. The tree with a knob like a bulbous nose, the creek curving around like the letter *S*, a patch of briars as tall as my shoulders. I lead Aarush left, right, around, and through, following the tugging in my belly that's pulling me deeper and deeper into the woods. The tree nose is oozing sap and the *S* creek is bigger than it was before, but I recognize the path.

Ouch. Aarush flinches. *Something thorny.*

It's gonna get worse, I'm sorry to say.

I figured, Aarush says.

And then it opens up into the clearing with his house.

Aarush nods. *And when we go inside, we don't split up, no matter what.*

Right, I say, nodding back.

While we can, before the trees get too thick, Aarush and I walk side by side. Our shoulders nearly touch, and we point our flashlights ahead of us, but even with the power of our double beams, the light doesn't really penetrate the dense woods. I try not to be spooked by every shadow, every gnarly face in the knobby bark of a tree, every rustle in the dry leaves and pine needles crunching under our feet.

We get closer and closer to the Fear Maker's house, and my breaths become a little shallower. I try to keep that sunflower feeling tucked between my ribs, but it's hard when the shadows are getting thicker and thicker, and the trees are pointing at you with bony hands.

At every turn, I imagine the beam from my flashlight landing on a waiting man: tall, red-eyed, eager. The trees seem to sneer as we struggle through them. I accidentally step into a spider's web, and the sticky strings break across my face. I flinch, then spit, in case I got any spidery string or blood-sucked insect carcasses in my mouth.

You okay? Aarush asks, hand on my elbow.

You bring any edible soap? I say, wiping my mouth.

Aarush pulls out the sunflower water bottle from his backpack, the one he brought just for me, and I take a swig.

Thanks, I say.

Come on, he says.

Soon, the woods get too dense for us to keep walking shoulder to shoulder. We have to squeeze through trees in single file, detangling our bodies from clinging branches that grip us like claws, sliding ourselves sideways between tall, scrawny tree trunks. I don't know how I manage it, but I go first. Dirt and sap under my fingernails, bloody scratches like battle wounds on my cheek, a tear in the sleeve of my favorite hoodie. Trees tell the scariest stories of all, with flashlights under their faces and wild, dry pine needles for a mane of hair.

I feel like I'm choking on my own heartbeat, but every time it feels like my pulse is going to burst through my skin, I slide my fingers into my pocket and trace over my stash of sunflower seeds.

Maybe you have power the Fear Maker can't even imagine, Grandma said.

Everything you need—it's all inside you already, the Gardener said.

I hope hope hope they're right.

They better be, because just then Aarush and I squeeze through the last cluster of bony branches that scrape my ribs, shiver my spine, block out the sky. We finally step through into the clearing where there are still no stars, only a vile, vile house.

A House

A

h o u s e

of   hunger.   A

house   that   stares   back.

A house pale as petrified wood, heartless,

though it seems to be breathing, lurking. A house waking from

the dead. A chimney reaches up like an arm reaching over our heads.

The eaves jut forward like the whole house is looking at us, throwing

shadows. Just us in	this clearing, Aarush
and me, no sounds but	our breathing and the
rasps of this foul,	step-halting house
made of creaking	boards and coffin
nails, of lightless	dirty windows that
still watch me, of	unswept porches
and rotting gabled	roofs. We step into
the soulless, watchful	clearing and I know
my night is about to	get so much worse.

Fire and Bone

I don't know how long Aarush and I stand there at the edge of the trees, frozen, staring. Neither of us wants to take the first step out into the open. Closer to that house.

And we thought the woods were bad.

The house is exactly as I saw it in my nightmare and in Aarush's drawing, but somehow even worse. As if nothing human could capture its sense of arrogance and malice, its flung-togetherness, like all of its bits and pieces morphed together in its own deviant sense of line and angle. A house without any kind of human touch, never meant for anything but fear.

And it seems even bigger since my last nightmare. Even more distorted and angled, like it's looming over our heads no matter how far away we're standing. Like the eyes in one of those trick portrait paintings that watch you wherever you move. I can't see anything through the dirty front window, and I wonder what is watching us from inside. My skin prickles, like every goose bump is being noticed by hungry eyes, and I feel like a wobbly wildebeest calf trying to square up against a hyena.

The trees on the sides of the house are withered and dead, but still seem ready to pull me up and hang me by my ankles given the slightest chance, leaving me dangling until

I'm nothing but bones. Seeing Aarush's face, it doesn't seem like he likes the look of this house much, either. Not much at all.

Do you smell that? Aarush asks.

Still staring at the house, I take a whiff. Despite the surreal and unnatural barrier of terror we just went through, my brain still expects to smell something natural, something like pine or soil and crushed leaves—but no. What I smell isn't that at all. I smell something like ammonia. Something like open wounds. A smell like I'm in a tight, too-small room with someone who's been sick and rotting for a very, very long time.

Oof, I say.

Oof, Aarush agrees.

I look up at the empty sky, where there really should be stars of some kind, but there are none. There is only a vast nothingness. The kind of nothingness that feels hovering and close, like the sky really could fall and crush you any second. Like maybe it's already rushing toward you.

Still, though, it's better than looking at that house.

Our parents are in there, Aarush says.

Yeah, I say.

I take Grandma's book of poems out from the drawstring bag over my shoulder. Just looking at her name, at the familiar words . . . I could use that right now. I open it to a random poem. But when I read the words on the page, they don't seem so random.

What is it? Aarush asks.

I clear my throat and read from Grandma's poem.

Here are the bones and living flames Hansel and Gretel turned against those who would consume them.

Wow, Aarush says.

Maybe that's why I couldn't go in last time—because I was going in alone. This house, though definitely not made of gingerbread and gumdrops, and hosting something even worse than a witch inside, is definitely one that would consume me. But maybe, together, Aarush and I can turn the nightmares against this monster. Maybe, together, we'll be strong enough to push this villain into his own oven, and thinking of Hansel and Gretel doing that to their witch is a better image to have in my head than any of the things I'm imagining we'll find once we walk through that door.

I listen to the night. Even a creepy owl or swooping bat would be comforting at this point—the unnatural quiet is worse. The only sounds are the whispers of wind in the crackling branches, and the squeak of the rocking chair on the front porch that's moving ever so slightly back and forth, back and forth.

Well, says Aarush. He holds up his hand, splaying his fingers. *I've got bones.*

I put the flashlight under my chin. *I've got flames.*

Maybe we're feeling a little frenzied, but for just a quick second we are laughing, there on the edge of the Fear Maker's clearing. Then, shoulder to shoulder again, Aarush and I face the house and take each other's hands. Not in a like-like way, but in a best-friend-who-I-am-very-very-glad-is-here-right-now kind of way.

And that way, terrified, hand in hand, we walk up the Fear Maker's front steps.

Knock Knock

So there we are. Standing on the Fear Maker's doorstep. Do we knock? Is the door already unlocked? I'm afraid to find out, and my hands are so cold they're beginning to hurt.

I turn to Aarush, ready to ask him what he thinks we should do, but then there's a creak. Slow and steady.

The door opens.

The door opens toward us like a claw, and the creaking hinges are outrageously loud in the silence.

Nobody is there. Just a blank, empty doorway leading into a house of shadow.

The doorframe seems just wide enough that Aarush and I could walk through together. The door opened like the house itself knew we were there. Knew we were coming. The only warmth comes from Aarush standing beside me.

We count to three, and together, we step inside.

It's even colder inside than out. I swear I can feel my terrified pulse in my fingertips. We take a few steps into the room, waiting for our eyes to adjust. Our flashlights seem much dimmer in here, tinted more pale green than yellow, like the light is pushing against tangible shadows. My beam barely seems to reach the corners. The dirty window is letting in zero light, and in fact I can hardly tell where it is.

Aarush and I stand back-to-back. I feel trembling, and I'm not sure if it's him or me. Probably both. My mind and heartbeat are racing with adrenaline, trying to prepare me for whatever's surely about to jump out from the shadows.

The front door slams.

Aarush and I scream. We point our lights at the front door, but it's not there. The door is gone. Nothing's there at all, just a blank wall.

Once we go in, we can't go back out.

I knew my nightmares were right.

I hate this already, Aarush says.

Me too, I say.

After a few deep breaths, after nothing pops out of the dark and nabs me, I make my way to where I thought the front door used to be. I put my hand along the wall, tracing cracks, looking for something, anything. My fingers find only solid cement that seems to be sucking the warmth from my skin. No sign at all of the missing door. When I turn away from where the door disappeared, I realize I don't see the smudgy window anywhere, either.

I look at Aarush in the dim light of our flashlights, and I think he's realizing the same thing. I keep waiting to see eyes staring at me from the corner. I keep waiting to hear the Fear Maker's voice from just behind me—Is he waiting, watching? Biding his time? It's Aarush who finally speaks.

Well. Then he clears his throat to hide a quivering voice. *Like my daada used to say, sometimes the only way out is through.*

I shine my light along each wall. The far wall, then the second, third, fourth. There are no windows and no doors.

Yeah, I say. *But where?*

Escape Room ABC's

A flashlight flickers.
Blank walls, four, all
cement. Impenetrable. No way out, no
doors, nothing here but us and an
eerie stillness. We start with the
floor, searching cracks and crevices,
going over every inch. A
hidden button or trapdoor, perhaps? No.
I move to the walls, feeling like a bug in a
jar. Like a rat, caught by the
king of malice. We
look in each corner, like mice in a
maze, searching for escape.
Nothing to find. How long until we lose courage,
or air? Aarush shivers, my
pulse is in my throat, and only getting
quicker. Aarush's light lands on a
rip in my jeans. _You're bleeding_, he
says. I look at my knee. The rim of the
tear is soaked in red. One drop of
umber blood hits the floor. Then the room, this
vault, rumbles. On the far

wall, a door slowly emerges. It yawns open
exactly like a mouth does, like a
yearning black hole, entrance to a lifeless dead
zone.

Stairway To...

Aarush and I stare at the new hole in the wall, at the doorway that morphed and emerged seemingly out of nowhere as soon as my blood touched the cement. This doorway is opposite where the front door should have been. Somehow it feels like we're standing in a monster's mouth, looking down into its esophagus, and I'm not sure that's entirely wrong. When I first saw it in my nightmares, I knew the Fear Maker's house was not quite inanimate.

A chill blows up from the open cavern. I pull my hoodie sleeves over my palms. I never did feel much pain from my torn-up knee—didn't even notice when I scraped it in the woods—and I don't feel much now except stiffness. Too much adrenaline in my veins, I think, making the blue lines along my wrists pop.

That's one trap room down, I suppose, Aarush says.

A trap we opened with blood. If this is just the first room, what will it take to get through the others? When the Gardener said the Fear Maker only twists and distorts—when he said I have everything I need inside me already—he couldn't have meant my blood?

We step up to the doorway like looking over a precipice. Together we shine our flashlights into the abyss.

Ahead of us is a staircase, going down. The walls are high, narrow, and the steps are steep. Our lights don't reach the bottom, the beams swallowed by the pitch black. My stomach drops like it's expecting someone to sneak up from behind us and push. Who knows how deep this staircase goes?

Aarush looks at me and holds up his fingers, wiggling them. *Bones*, he says.

My throat clutches, and I feel like courage is dripping out of me along with the blood on my scraped-up knee, but I hold up my flashlight. *Flames*, I say.

We go down onto the first step.

There is a loud creak, because of course there is. We take another step. Is the Fear Maker waiting at the bottom of these stairs? Why hasn't he shown up already? Is he watching us? I can easily imagine him enjoying our struggle, laughing at our pathetic attempts to beat him, to finish his maze.

How deep is that room where my parents' souls are being held captive?

As we walk, we find a rhythm, going down each step together, right, left, right, left. For a long while, the beams from our flashlights still don't reach the bottom step, and my skin is goosebumping in the cold.

I blink, and then there's the bottom of the stairs. Aarush and I both stop. After our grave, rhythmic marching, suddenly coming across the bottom of the staircase takes us both off guard.

I shine my beam on the last step and slowly move the light upward. There's a door. A gray wooden door with faded, peeling paint and a large gold doorknob. Deep in the wood, etched into the peeling paint, I think there are scratch marks.

I move my beam to the right of the door and nearly drop

my flashlight. There's a chair there, and in it, a slumped, cloaked figure.

I swallow back another scream. Aarush grabs my wrist. He must notice it, too. We wait, but the figure doesn't budge. All we can see is the long black cloak draped over its shoulders and flowing to the floor. The hood is pulled far over its head. The figure sits stiffly, like it's been slumped in this chair for a very, very long time.

Was that a ripple in the cloak? A breath, in and out? Or was that a trick of our flickering flashlights?

After an age of waiting, when the figure still doesn't move, we take the last few steps down to the bottom. My stomach clenches. Whoever's in that chair will suddenly look up at me, I'm sure. There's going to be those blank white eyes, staring. This has got to be one of the Fear Maker's traps, though I don't think it's the monster himself. I can feel him close and getting nearer, but this doesn't seem like him.

Then we're standing right in front of the chair.

I try to speak, but only a tiny whimper comes through my cardboard throat. I clear it.

Hello? I whisper.

Nothing.

Hello? We're going to go through this door, okay? I say.

Again, nothing.

So Aarush steps forward and taps the figure's shoulder. Nothing. He taps again, harder, and when he does, the figure's head rolls backward and the hood falls away and what stares back at us is a hollow-eyed, white-toothed skull.

I scream and back away. Aarush does, too, and in that second we're both pressed against the opposite wall, those empty sockets turned toward us. Icy panic trickles down each of my vertebrae.

Finally, my hyperventilation settles down a little bit. Even after all that, the skeleton figure still hasn't moved, though in this place, I wouldn't be surprised if it could.

I hear Aarush gulp. *At least it doesn't look like it's going to stop us from going through that door*, he says.

I nod. When I can unfreeze my limbs, I step forward, staying as far away from the grinning skull as possible. I twist the knob. When it doesn't budge, my stomach drops.

It's locked, I say.

I feel like sliding to the floor, burying my head in my knees, and sobbing. Already I feel defeated by something as stupid as a locked door, and who knows how much farther we have to go. How much farther to Mom and Dad and all the others. How many more locked doors do we have ahead?

I think . . . Aarush says, hesitating. He looks back and forth between the door and the skeleton figure. *I think this skeleton dude has something to do with getting through the door.*

The skull's cavernous eyes are doors to a hollow emptiness.

Unfortunately, I think you're right, I say.

So I take a deep breath and we step forward, leaning more closely over the skeleton in its cloak.

Do you think . . . ? With my fingertips, like I'm picking up a used tissue, I pull the cloak open, revealing the full skeleton underneath. The rib cage is empty, like a birdcage with no birds. I check for anything tied around the skeleton's neck. Keys on a string are a thing sometimes, aren't they? But there's nothing.

It's so dark down here. Our lights barely illuminate us and the bones. I stop myself from looking back up the stairs, because I keep imagining something or someone at the top of them, looking down at us, watching. If I looked up and saw anything there, I think my heart really would give out. No, I have to focus. Focus on the morbid, gruesome bone-search.

Penny, Aarush says.

I wonder if there are pockets, I say, crouching down by the cloak.

Penny, Aarush says again.

I look up at him. His eyes are wide, staring. I look where his light is pointing.

Aarush has rolled up the skeleton's sleeves. A good thought, since the skeleton could be gripping the key, even in death. But that's not what Aarush found. Not exactly. The skeleton hand is draped over the front curve of the armrest, its bony fingers in a grip. Its right pointer finger is extra long, extra thin, and at the very tip, shaped like the shaft of a key.

I stand up fast, away from the grotesque hand.

Ugh.

Yeah, Aarush says.

On instinct, I tuck my hands under my armpits, like I'm trying to protect them. *Who is this guy, do you think?*

I have no idea, Aarush says. *Someone the Fear Maker got? Or . . . what if someone* wanted *to be here, with the Fear Maker?*

That thought is too horrible. *Maybe if he can make this house, he can make bones, too?*

Yeah, maybe, Aarush says.

I gulp. *So we...*

Yeah.

No. No way. I step back again.

Aarush stares at the bone-key. His gentle roundness is the antithesis of the sharp, threatening skeleton in front of us. He inhales deeply, then exhales so slowly it comes out almost a whistle.

Hold on, Mom and Dad, he whispers, so softly I barely hear. Then in one quick motion he reaches out, grabs that long, misshapen finger, and with a loud, sickening crack, breaks it off from the hand.

He wobbles the tiniest bit when he stands up straight, and his cheeks are ashen, like he's fighting off nausea. But he takes a determined step toward the locked, scratched-up door. He puts the bone-key into the lock.

It fits perfectly.

Hickory Dickory Dock

Hickory Dickory Dock
The bone-key fits the lock
Who was it that died
So we'd come inside?
Hickory Dickory Dock

What's Behind Door Number...

Another door. Another opening into shadow. What if there is only door after door, going deeper and deeper, no end in sight, until we're both driven out of our minds? How am I supposed to use poems and sunflower seeds in a place like this? If the Gardener is right and the Fear Maker can't create like I can, then what about this monstrous house, its trapdoors, and its twisted rooms? How did he create all of this?

Aarush nudges me. My face must have betrayed my thoughts, because he says, *Onward. We got this.*

I'm not as convinced as I hope he is, but I nod.

We step together through the next doorway.

As our feet touch the ground on the other side, automated lights flicker on with a click. Bright lights, harsh, the long tube kind like the ones in hospitals and scuzzy apartments. The sudden brightness makes me squint, and I hold my hand up like the visor on a baseball cap. Slowly, my eyes start to adjust.

We are at the end of a long, long hallway. As with the stairs, the light doesn't reach the far end of the corridor, and it goes on and on into shadow. Doors line each side of the hallway, each numbered with a metallic gold number like in a motel. The walls are papered in a faded, mustardy yellow with a circular design that looks like eyes. The designs on one wall seem a fraction closer together than normal eyes, and on the other, a fraction too far apart.

The hall is lined with carpeting, a swirly maroon carpet that might once have been rich, but now looks worn. The swirls and frills come darkest out from under each door, like each room bled out the design.

What are we supposed to do now? I ask. *Are we supposed to look in every room? Are we supposed to choose one?*

I step into the hallway, looking at the golden number to my right. I lean in, putting my ear to the door. I can't hear anything on the other side, but that doesn't mean nothing's there. No peephole in the door to look through.

What would the Gardener tell me?

What about door number seven? Aarush says. He looks uncertain, but at least it's a suggestion. I remember the story Aarush told me about his great-grandfather, what he told me about the seven seeds and our ancestors guiding us sometimes. I'm about to say, *Sure, yeah, we might as well start somewhere*, but just then the door behind us, the one we came through, slams shut with a loud, echoing clap. We jump and turn around.

Standing there at the entrance to the hallway, in front of the closed door, is the skeleton.

Slowly, slowly, the skeleton raises its arm. The robes hang from its bones like the sweeping cloak of a Grim Reaper. The skeleton stretches out its hand and points at us with its thin, broken finger.

SEVEN! I yell. *SEVEN IS GOOD.*

And we run.

We book it down the hall, and out of the corner of my eye I see the skeleton lurching after us. I swear the eyes on the wallpaper are watching us, too. One of the bulbs above us flickers, then fizzes out. As the skeleton chases us, its bones creak and its teeth click-clack together with each jolting step.

As we home in on door number seven, I pray with every cell in my body, on every seed from every sunflower, that the knob will turn.

It does. I nearly break with relief.

The skeleton has almost reached us. I shove open the door with all my might, and Aarush and I practically fall over the threshold. We push the door shut behind us just as the skeleton reaches it, and we press both our weights against the door, trying to close it against the skeleton pushing back. Aarush grunts and we give the door one final heave.

It closes.

The sleeve of the skeleton's cloak is trapped under the latch. After a moment of tugging, the skeleton frees its sleeve. The skeleton bangs several times on the door, hard, and I feel the door tremble. I'm relieved for a second when the banging stops, but then the scratching starts.

Slow, deep scratching on the other side of the door that I swear I can feel in my own spine, and that's even worse. Aarush seems just as frozen in place as I am while we wait for the noise to stop. Finally, finally, it does, and with our ears to the door, Aarush and I listen to the bones rattle their way back down the hall.

Both of our chests are heaving, and it takes a minute for me to recover. When he's caught his breath, Aarush looks at me. *I guess we're going with door number seven*, he says.

We turn around.

This Room

Light switch.
Turn on.
Four walls,
dingy cement,
three covered
in writing—
countless words
scribbled hard,
letters crammed.
Bare floor,
no bed,
no door.
The chandelier
is made
of hands;
fingers splayed
and cupped
around bright
bulbs. But
the last
wall, across
from us
has no
writing. No,

it's overgrown
with full-lipped
wide
gaping
mouths.

Use Your Words

Oh, come ON, Aarush says.

We stare at the wall of mouths, dozens and dozens of mouths.

Some are open, with white teeth or chipped yellow ones. Some are frowning, some are in a closed-mouth grin. I see baby lips, and goth lips painted black, chapped lips, wrinkled lips, lips with orange gloss. There's even one grinning mouth with braces on its teeth, and one with a missing tooth. A few mouths move like they're whispering, but no sound emerges.

That is . . . really creepy, Aarush says.

Yeah, I say.

I gulp, now overly conscious of my dry lips, and the way my tongue feels behind my teeth.

A wall of mouths.

If I screamed, would they smile? If I cried, would they laugh?

I look back over my shoulder. As before in this house of horrors, the door is gone. Disappeared. It's just us, four walls, and those mouths.

And the writing.

The letters all seem written furiously, in both the speed and the anger sense. I see lines scribbled in hard letters I can barely distinguish, blobs of ink. Dripping down the wall like blood.

I say, *There's got to be some kind of clue in the words.*

Yeah, good thinking, Aarush says.

We look closer at the thick letters covering the three walls. The hand chandelier casts finger shadows over the writing.

The sentences all seem to blur together. It's hard to even make out where one word ends and the next begins, which is why I've gone over almost an entire wall before it hits me.

Oh my gosh, I say. *Aarush.*

What? he asks.

Holy crap.

What? What is it?

I look at Aarush. Is it just me, or are more of the mouths grinning now?

These are my words, I say, pointing at the wall. *These are my poems.*

Aarush's mouth drops open. *No way.*

Yeah. In someone else's murdery handwriting, but yeah.

Aarush turns in a slow circle, looking over the words. *You wrote all this? All these poems?*

There are so many bigger things going on, but it still feels a little strange to suddenly have Aarush reading my work when this wasn't at all what I was planning on. But I give him a nervous smile. *Blame my grandma. Poetry is genetic, I guess.*

We both manage a tiny smile. Grandma is a good thought to have right now.

Okay, he says. *So what do we do? How are we supposed to get out this time?*

I have no idea. I knew I should have written a poem about how to escape the haunted lair of an evil monster.

Never ignore inspiration, Penny. Aarush is pale, but he grins. Hallelujah for jokes, carrying us onward. What would I have done if Aarush wasn't here?

I'll be sure and write one for next time, I say.

Ugh, don't even say the words "next time."

No kidding.

We've got to try something, so I square my shoulders, muster any crumbs of courage I can, give my sunflower seeds in my pocket a pat, and step forward.

Listen up, I say, hoping these mouths can hear me. *We need to get out of this room. How do we do it?*

I wait for a moment. Silence.

Hey, I say, stepping closer. *I said—*

The mouths all open at once as I walk ahead, like they can sense me nearby. They're still silent, but they open and close, open and close, like waiting baby birds. Baby birds waiting for their mama bird to bring them a meal.

Ew, I say. *I think they're hungry.*

That's terrifying, Aarush says. But he puts down his backpack and unzips it. *Let's see if they like granola bars, then.*

He pulls one out from his backpack, unwraps the plastic, and approaches the wall of mouths. At first they part open and closed, open and closed, for him, too, but as he holds up the granola bar to the first pair of lips, they close tight and firm.

Come on, Aarush says, holding the food closer. The lips clench tighter.

He tries a different mouth, the one with braces. That mouth, too, closes against the food. He tries another mouth, and another, and each time it's the same. There are at least three or four dozen mouths on the wall, and every single one refuses the granola bar.

What do you think they want? he says.

Our presence has definitely woken them up or something, because apart from Aarush trying to shove a granola bar through their lips, the mouths keep doing the hungry-bird thing, opening and closing.

Do you think . . . ? I say.

Like the floor upstairs? he says.

We're thinking the same thing.

Man, I really hope not, I say. I look down at my scabbing knee. The bleeding has mostly stopped, but our running from the skeleton must have opened up the deepest cuts a bit, because I'm able to get a little smear of blood on my finger.

I hate this, I say.

Me too, Aarush says.

Still, I step forward and hold out my bloody finger to the mouth with the black lipstick.

My lungs exhale pure relief when the lips close up tight.

I try another mouth just in case. Again, a no-go.

So they're not cannibals, Aarush says. *That's . . . good.*

I wipe my finger on the hem of my jeans and turn back to the scribbles on the wall. The answer must be there somewhere.

After careful reading, I find what I recognize to be the first line of one of my old poems. It's smooshed up against the previous lines and hard to distinguish. I scan through the words, looking for the poem's end.

Hey, wait a sec.

Got something? Aarush says.

I think so, yeah. I think . . . yeah, one of the words in this poem is wrong.

I point to the words a little above our heads, on the wall where the door should have been.

See right there? Where it says "bury yourself"?

It takes Aarush a moment, but he finds it. He mumbles words to himself, then louder when he finds the right line.

*"And when the monsoon rages, use stones and bury yourself."
You wrote that?*

It's supposed to be "brace yourself," I say.

Brace yourself?

Yeah.

Then Aarush's eyes go wide, and his brow lifts with the huge, rising, hot-air balloon of an idea.

Brace like braces? he says.

Huh?

Is that poem with you? he says. *In your notebook?*

Yeah, I'm pretty sure all of them are. Why?

What if they . . . no, never mind, it's stupid.

That's when I catch on. Aarush sees the same idea clicking into place behind my eyes.

At the same time, we say, *What if they eat poetry?*

And, I say, the idea building on itself brick by brick, *and the wrong words tell us which poem goes with which mouth.*

Yes! Aarush says, jumping a little with excitement.

Quickly as I can, I swing my drawstring bag from my

shoulders and pull out my notebook. There are a lot of words in this notebook with the Van Gogh sunflower cover. Some words could maybe one day turn into something. Some were never meant to be seen by another soul.

I flip the notebook open to the "brace yourself" poem. My fingers grip the top of the page, ready to rip, but I hesitate. Am I really about to tear up my notebook?

Aarush can tell what I'm thinking.

Hey, he says. *I'm sorry about this, and I know it sucks. But remember, there's infinity more where that came from*, and he gives my head a little tap.

I smile in spite of myself. *Thanks*, I say. Is sacrificing these poems worth fighting this fight and getting my parents back? I know the answer without having to think any more about it, and with one swift tug I tear out the page.

This time, when I bring the page to the mouth with the braces, the lips part and the mouth opens wide wide wide. It feels so personal, feeding out my poetry like this. Almost more personal than if the mouths in the wall actually did want my blood. But it's like Aarush said: There's more where these came from. Unlike blood, I think to myself, poetry doesn't diminish when you give it away. It doesn't even leave you. Not really. Poetry will always be there.

Maybe if we survive all this, I'll write a poem about that.

So I hold out the page with my words written on it. The mouth takes the paper between its teeth, nibbles it smaller and smaller like a rabbit chewing a cabbage leaf. It nibbles until the page is gone. Then the lips curl in on themselves and suck back into the wall until suddenly, the mouth with the braces is gone, leaving an empty spot of bare cement.

Okay, then, Aarush says.

I feel myself shift into a higher gear. Now I'm in a hurry. Now that we know how to get out of this awful room, I want to get through this as quickly as possible. If we can de-mouth the wall, we're one step closer to finishing the Fear Maker's maze. One step closer to Mom and Dad.

I rip two of the less embarrassing poems from my notebook.

Here, I say, hurriedly handing them to Aarush. *Look for these ones.*

Aarush takes the pages and nods. I take a couple of pages for myself, a couple of the ones I'd rather nobody else see. I look from page to wall, page to wall, trying to find a match.

I know this isn't the right time, Aarush says, looking at my pages. *But you're really good.*

I look down at my sunflower notebook cover. *Thanks,* I say. *Keep looking.*

And so for the next several minutes we work in silence. It takes a bit of time, but soon we get into the rhythm. Soon we start finding matches.

Got one, Aarush says. He holds up one of the pages, comparing it to words near the top of the left wall. *The wall says "mauve" where you wrote "orange."*

He turns to the mouth wall and spots the lips with bright orange gloss. The lips part wide, devour the page, and then they, too, curl in on themselves and disappear into the wall.

We find more and more matches. Words like *wrinkled* and

gothic. Plump for the fullest lips, *melancholy* for the deepest frown. It takes a lot of time and effort to find just one match, and when the process seems the most tedious, we try feeding a blank page to one of the mouths just to see what happens. They chew the blank page down greedily, but afterward, the lips remain. They only disappear into the wall if we've matched them with the right poem. No shortcuts out of this room, I guess.

Finally, we're down to just a few mouths left. We match the word *packed* to a mouth with teeth jammed over themselves, and *remains* to a mouth with something like spinach caught in its teeth. Each time the mouths curl in on themselves and pop back into the wall, I feel my stomach roil.

Then there's only one mouth left. The small baby lips, smack-dab in the center of the wall.

What words haven't we used? I say, looking around.

I think those ones. I've been trying to keep track. Aarush points at some scribbles near the floorboard. I read through the words, and when I realize what they are, I can't help but laugh.

Oh my gosh, I say. *It's the first poem I ever wrote. Years ago. Before the . . . before I got scared of showing people my work. Obviously, it's not in my notebook, but I remember it.* I look at the words again. *And they're missing the whole last line.*

So I turn to a blank page in my notebook. I write out the poem from memory . . . *Roses aren't red. Violets aren't blue.* Then I add the missing last line. My heart feels a little tender looking at my first meager and overeager efforts at verse. Grandma kept the poem on the fridge for years.

This is it. I'm coming, Mom and Dad. I gently hold the page out to the baby lips. Like the others, this mouth eats the poem right up. But this time, instead of disappearing, the mouth slowly starts to grow. It grows and opens, opens and grows, until the bottom lip reaches the floor. The throat gets taller and taller until the esophagus looks like a dark, damp hallway. Soon, the open mouth is wide enough to walk through.

The First Poem I Ever Wrote

Roses aren't red.
Violets aren't blue.
They're a million colors each
like a sky you fall through.

Sunflowers feel yellow
because of their faces.
Lilies go dancing
in all sorts of places.

Your feet will get dirty
but there's lots to see
when you come to visit
my garden and me.

Winner Winner Chicken Dinner

We step together into the open mouth. I put my depleted notebook back in my bag and try to focus on the flickering orange glow ahead of us, and not on the teeth closing shut behind, or the soft squishy something we're walking on. (I am trying *so* hard not to think about exactly what it is that we're walking on, but I keep imagining the feel of tiny shoes walking across my own tongue and down the back of my throat.)

Then we're at the end of the dark, wet tunnel. We step through a square of light into a large room lit with ornate sconces and firelight. In fact, the fire is behind us, as if we've just come down the chimney and out of the fireplace. There's a second fireplace across the room as well. The soft ground below us is a lush red carpet.

In the center of the room is a large wooden table, packed with the hugest feast I've ever seen—roast beef and ham, piles of mashed potatoes, broccoli and cauliflower drizzled with cheese, platters filled with grapes and berries.

And there, standing at the other side of the table, are our parents.

My brain struggles to catch up with what I'm seeing. Mom? Dad? Here? Already? Did we win?

Where's the Fear Maker?

Beside me, Aarush lets out a choked sob, a sound that comes from deep between his ribs. *Mom*, he says. He rushes

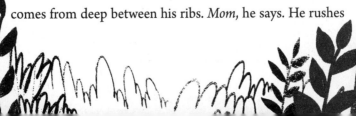

forward, stumbling, nearly knocking over a pitcher of apple cider in his hurry to the other side of the table.

While Aarush flings his arms around his mom's waist, his dad's arms wrapped around them both, I slowly make my own way around the table to where my parents are smiling at me.

Mom? Dad?

Hi, sweetie, Mom says.

Did we make it? How are you here?

Of course you made it, Dad says.

I check their eyes. Normal, it seems. At least not empty and blank, like before. In fact, their eyes seem extra bright in the firelight. The skin around their eyes seems smoother. Fewer worry lines and wrinkles.

Where have you been? I say, fighting the heat growing behind my eyes.

Dad pulls me into a hug and I lean against his chest.

Waiting for you, he says.

Is this really it?

I inhale, looking for that floral, earthy scent that inevitably makes its way into all my dad's clothes. But this shirt smells clean. It smells of nothing at all, really. Maybe it's new?

I step back and look at my mom. She puts a hand on my head, stroking my hair.

Questions keep seeping in at the edges of my brain, like drips from a leaky faucet. I'm still confused, and each drip is a reminder of something else that doesn't make sense. What about the Fear Maker? What about the door at the heart of the house? Where is everyone else he devoured? I want so badly to just be done with this whole nightmare, to have someone else finally take care of everything, but the questions keep coming. They keep drip-dripping into my mind, so I ask the most desperate one.

Can we go home now?

Mom laughs, an oddly hard laugh like clinking crystals. *Of course, sweetie,* she says. *But don't you want to eat something first? You must be starving, and we made all this for you.*

Aarush's parents must be telling him the same thing, because his dad pulls out a chair and Aarush slides into it. His parents take the seats on either side, and Aarush's mom starts dishing up, filling his plate with heaping spoonfuls of everything. She cuts him off a thick slice of roast.

Didn't Aarush say they don't eat meat, especially red meat? Is this an extenuating circumstance?

My parents usher me to the other side of the table and seat me between them, opposite Aarush.

I desperately want not to admit it, but my stomach is burbling with uncertainty. Something is really off.

Mom starts piling my plate high, too.

Hey, Dad, I say, gulping. Please let everything be okay. Please let the Fear Maker be gone. *What's your favorite flower today?* I ask.

Dad gives me a full-tooth grin. *Oh, I couldn't pick,* he says. *They're all great.*

No. *Dad, please.*

You, he says, patting my head. *You're my favorite flower, Penelope.*

Oh, Dad. No, no.

He turns to his plate.

Eat up, Mom says to me.

Across from me, Aarush is lifting a spoonful of potatoes to his mouth.

Aarush, stop! I shout, louder than I intended.

Aarush's spoon freezes.

Have you eaten anything? I say.

What? No, not yet. Why? What's going on?

These aren't them. I try to speak but my voice is a hoarse whisper.

What?

I blink back that awful heat in my eyes. Clear my throat. *These aren't them. These are not our parents.*

My dad's hand on my shoulder turns into a grip. I jump up from my chair before his hold can get any tighter.

Of course we're your parents, he says.

Of course we are, Mom says. She also stands up from her chair. She leans in toward me. *You're just tired, sweetie.*

What are you talking about? Aarush is looking at me hard, almost glaring. His voice is steely with anger, and I don't blame him. Everything about this is cruel, and this might not have happened to his parents if it wasn't for me. But he has to believe me. He has to. I can't leave him here. He'll die, or worse. How could I finish the maze—confront the Fear Maker—without him?

Aarush, please, I say. *Think about it. I know it sucks, but think. Look at your plate.*

He looks down at his food. At the thick slice of roast, its juices seeping over everything. He looks at his mom. He looks at her for a long time. She looks down at him, grinning too wide.

It's . . . it's . . . He's trying to deny it, like I want to. Trying to find excuses. Because finally finding our parents, but then not, is too much to bear. Like piling brick after brick into our backpacks.

When Aarush looks back up at me, his eyes are puffed and brimming with tears. He looks at his mom and dad again.

No, he says.

Aarush, I say.

Then he swears, loud and hard, and slams his spoon down, splattering mashed potatoes everywhere. I'm afraid the curse was meant for me, terrified he's been caught in this trap I've dragged him into, but with teeth clenched he says, *I'm going to shove this freaking spoon down the Fear Maker's freaking throat.*

Aarush, son, his dad says, reaching out a hand. But Aarush flinches and pushes the hand away. He scurries out from between his fake parents and over to me. His hands are clenched in white-knuckle fists, a couple of tears escaping down his cheeks.

The four Not-Parents start walking toward us, smiling like wolves.

Calm down, Aarush's Not-Mom says. *You've been through a lot.*

You're just confused, says my Not-Mom. *Come eat and rest.*

I look around the room frantically, searching for a way out. There are no doors or windows here, either. There's the table, the fireplace we came through plus the second one in the opposite wall, and several portraits of fancy people hanging up high. All the painted faces look wide-eyed, like the people haven't blinked in a long time. There are dozens of antlers and dead animal heads mounted between the portraits. Raccoons, moose, cougars, each with their teeth showing. I didn't notice any of this before. It's like there was a haze put on my thoughts, distracting me from seeing anything but what I wanted to see—my parents—in this part of the Fear Maker's twisted, twisted maze. But now that I *have* noticed, the more I notice and the more ominous and unreal it all seems.

What do we do? Aarush whispers. I think he's finally noticing the doorless situation, too.

Another Fear Maker trap we have to escape.

When I speak, I don't bother to whisper. It's not about outwitting whoever these fakes are anymore, it's about getting away. No different from escaping the finger-key skeleton.

It's gotta be the other fireplace, I say. *One to come in, one to go out. If we can make it.*

But the fire, he says. As he does, the flames in the exit flue billow higher.

The four fake parents take another slow step toward us.

Come here, Penny, says my Not-Dad.

You are not my dad, I say. *And you're not my mom.*

Of course we are, my Not-Mom says.

Get away from me, Aarush screams at his fake mom. *Where's my real mom?*

I'm right here, says the fake.

You are not real, Aarush says. *You are not real.*

It's like a chant, and I join in.

You are not real. You are not real.

As we say the words louder and louder, the four creatures walking toward us begin to change. Their too-bright eyes begin to glow red. Their smiles open, revealing sharp teeth. I watch my mom's and dad's faces morph and change until all I see are monsters wearing masks.

I grab Aarush's hand.

The fireplace! I yell again. I pull him away from the creatures and around the table, so that the table is between us and the fake parents. I grab the bowl of potatoes and throw it with all my might, hitting my fake dad's shoulder, but it doesn't deter him. All the monsters keep advancing, their wolfy grins even bigger. I pull Aarush harder toward the fireplace.

But the fire! The fire! Aarush says. The closer we get, the higher the flames reach. The blaze is squint-bright, and I can feel the heat licking my skin.

If those things aren't really our parents, I say, *then that's not really a fire.*

As we dash into the flames, the sharp-toothed, glowing-eyed fake parents right behind us, I really hope I'm right.

Not Fair

We run through flames.
The touch is bitter cold, not hot.
More like dry ice—
like an imitation fire built
by someone who's never felt warm.

It's not fair.

On the other side of fire,
Aarush collapses to his knees.
Can't catch his breath.
Chest heaving with Mariana-deep sobs,
fingers tearing up grass in clumps.

<u>It's not fair,</u>

he says. <u>He can't use
my parents like that.</u>
I kneel beside him,
my hand on his back, feel the angry
beat of his heart through his shirt.

<u>It's not fair.</u>

It's heavy, infuriating, exhausting, and I am so tired.

We sit together, breathing. The tide
   of Aarush's crashing grief
ebbs a little. Then dirt and grass finally register.
A night sky. Flashing carnival lights ahead,
swirling neon, and even faint, tinkling music.

Where are we?

The Not-Fair

When he's ready, Aarush inhales as deep as grief will let him and gives me a slight nod. We stand up and face the flashing bulbs and grating, tinny music in the distance. It took a minute to get situated after what just happened, but now that I'm looking around, I feel my stomach drop thinking about having to face whatever the Fear Maker's got under those neon lights. The Fear Maker seed in my gut wriggles. Like it's excited.

There is grass under our feet, a starless sky above, and even, if I concentrate, the briefest of breezes. But the grass doesn't look quite right. The same unreal color as the grass in the Fear Maker's clearing. As desperately as I wish we were really outside and out of the Fear Maker's house, I don't believe it. I think the grass, the dirt, the sky, the outside, is all an imitation. Counterfeit. Fake like the fire we just went through, like the fake parents and their fake food and their fake smiles.

My sunflower seeds—not fake—are comfortingly secure in my pocket, worn smooth by the rubbing of my thumb. I close my eyes and think of the smell of the Gardener's coat, the richness of the yellow in each and every sunflower petal. I think of Grandma reading me poems at night, and my true Mom and Dad in here, somewhere.

I think of Real.

I open my eyes.

I think we're still inside the Fear Maker's house, I say. *I think this is all a facade.*

Aarush wipes his eyes on the sleeve of his hoodie and takes a deep breath in that lifts his shoulders, and a deep breath out that lasts for lots of seconds.

Yes, he says. *I think so, too.*

It's clear where we need to go. I nod in the direction of the creepy lights.

Okay? I say. Even though none of this is actually okay.

Aarush nods.

Together we start walking toward the lights. We don't walk for long. We reach them quicker than I expected—quicker than we should have been able to if this place were real, if it was made of anything more than nightmare.

An animatronic clown face with exaggerated red lips and sharp blue triangles over its eyes laughs at us as we walk through the entrance into the fair. Its face is lit with wild neon colors. Its eyes swirl and its teeth chomp. We walk down the main aisle. Nobody else is here. Not a single person. The lights are on, the rides and games are going, but we're the only people.

It's like the Fear Maker took the quintessential idea of a carnival and fed it poison.

Speaking of Not-Fair, I say.

He's evil. Aarush's face is still flushed and angry.

Remind me to take you to Pumpkin Joe's next year, I say. *There's a chance you'll like it better.*

If we make it out of this, Aarush says.

It's the first and only time Aarush has expressed any doubt about us surviving this ordeal, and it's like the echo of an earthquake has passed under my feet.

I don't quite know how to respond, except to keep us moving forward down the aisle.

The music is just a fraction off-key. It sounds as if it's coming from old, worn-out speakers, but I don't see the speakers anywhere, as if the music is playing from the sky itself.

There's a smell of kettle corn that, if I concentrate on it too hard, begins to smell like puke. The flashing lights and twirling games seem to beckon, trying to call us over.

On our right is a carousel. It turns slowly, slowly, and the horse's wide eyes shimmer. The pipes squeak as the horses lift up and down, up and down. After watching for a moment, I notice that all the horses' teeth look too white and too big for their mouths.

Farther into the fair, on our left, is a booth that lets you shoot water at moving targets. The targets, dancing on their sticks, are painted faces. Although nobody is sitting at the counter or lined up to play, one of the guns jets out water that hits one of the faces smack in the head. The water coming from the gun looks red.

There is a small red-and-white-striped tent with a *Hall of Mirrors* sign hanging above the flap. I don't want to look, but as we pass, I catch a glimpse of myself in one of the mirrors. In my reflection, my whole face is an empty space. No eyes, nose, or mouth at all, just a blank fleshy nothing.

We keep walking. There's a booth lined with marionettes that seem to be watching us as we walk past. Blinking lights throw shadows everywhere, and the music seems to be getting louder.

We reach the end of the path and stand in front of the entrance to the ride at the edge of the fair. The big one. We both stare at the sign for a second.

Great, Aarush says. *Just great.*

The archway ahead of us is flanked by two torches belching huge spurts of fire. Unlike the rest of the fair, everything beyond the archway is unlit, kept in shadow, though high above us I see the silhouette of a roller-coaster loop.

Across the archway, written in sharp, serial-killer-style font, is the name of the ride: *The Fear Maker.*

I gulp.

I don't think this is just a ride, either. I think this is what will take us to the middle of the Fear Maker's maze. To the monster himself.

I'm pretty sure he'll be waiting on the other side of this thing, I tell Aarush.

The off-key music sounds like it's playing right over our heads. In the flicker of the swirling neon bulbs, the writing over the roller-coaster sign almost looks like it's slithering.

Why did this have to happen? Aarush says suddenly, looking about ready to punch the sign itself. *My parents didn't do anything.*

I'm sorry, I say. *I don't know what to say.*

I hate this. I hate him. How dare he.

I'm really sorry, I say. I've never seen Aarush like this. He jitters like his skin doesn't feel right with all this bitterness bubbling inside. I feel panic foaming up in me like soda fizz, because what if this is his breaking point? I know what to expect from regular Aarush, but hurt, enraged Aarush? I'm afraid he'll decide he's done, over it, gone. I'm afraid he'll start turning that contempt against the person who brought him here . . .

I'm not a hateful person. I'm not. I don't want to be. But ugh. Aarush's hands are clenched in white-knuckle fists.

I know you're not, I say, getting more and more frantic myself the deeper Aarush's spiral goes.

I want to hurt him. I . . . I want to hurt him and I've never wanted to hurt anyone before.

I know, but, Aarush—

Did he get to them because of where we live? he asks. *Because we live nearby?* His toe digs into the ground, making an angry little divot in the dirt. *Is it because I'm friends with you?*

And then we both freeze.

Aarush's stormy squirming stops. He looks at me, eyes wide and stunned.

My stomach is in my heels, and I wish it was a lead ball that would pull me deep, deep underground.

I didn't mean that. Aarush's whole face is pale with guilt. *I am so sorry, Penny. I really didn't mean that.*

He steps toward me, and I flinch. All my fault, all my fault.

Penny, I should not have said that. It's not what I really think at all. I just . . . this place. This awful, awful place.

I swallow. I brought him here. I caused this. I can't let the Fear Maker take him away from me, too. I can't I can't I can't.

Aarush's eyes glint with wetness and the shimmer of the neon bulbs. His voice chokes. *And he used my mom.*

That's it, the deepest bruise. Maybe the deepest hurt he's ever felt, and I understand. That's what this is about, not him blaming me. That's the truth. It takes a moment, but the muscles in my shoulders slowly release their tension. I nod. *It's okay*, I say.

Penny, he says. *I don't regret doing this, as awful as it is. I don't regret coming with you.*

I nod. *Thanks*, I say.

I'm really sorry, he says.

I understand. You're right about this place. It . . . it messes you up.

We both take a deep breath.

Then we should probably get going and figure out how in the world we get out of here, Aarush says.

To literally anywhere else.

Someplace nicer, he says. *Like prison.*

Yep, I say.

Neither of us moves.

Ever been on a loop roller coaster? Aarush says, looking at the shadowy track looming in the distance.

Nope, I say. *I hate roller coasters.*

Same, he says.

My legs—every part of me—really don't want to move. It's as if even my feet know for themselves that this is it. The final walk into the deepest shadows. The last ride to The End.

Well, there's a first time for everything, Aarush says.

And a last time, too, I think, but at least Aarush is sounding a little more like himself. I force my frozen feet to move, and together we step toward the roller coaster. Toward the Fear Maker.

As we step forward, more torches on either side of us burst into life, lighting the next few yards. The first time it happens, it makes me flinch, but with each step, more torches illuminate our path to the ride. New shadows pop up with every new torch.

Finally, a last light flashes on. This time it's a giant spotlight, pointed to a set of wooden steps that lead up to a wooden platform and the roller-coaster tracks. Dust particles dance in the harsh spotlight, and the world beyond the illuminated circle looks even dimmer.

As we watch, an empty roller-coaster train slowly, slowly pulls into the light. The coaster cars are a shiny orange, with two glowing red eyes painted on the front. The train inches its way forward like an eel, then creaks to a halt. With a puff like a deflating tire, the shoulder restraints pop open.

I look at Aarush. We don't have to say it out loud because we're both thinking the same thing: Getting into that creepy, death-trap roller-coaster car is the only way we might possibly be able to save our parents. I'm not sure I like our chances. I feel like my hope has shrunk to just one tiny little match inside me, hardly enough to light a single step.

But I look at Aarush and he gives my hand a quick squeeze.

The only way out is through, he says.

I nod, and squeeze his hand back.

We step up the stairs.

One step up for our parents.

One step up for all the others taken by the Fear Maker.

One step up for the two of us, and the kind of people we better be if we're going to beat this thing.

We reach the loading platform.

Okay, Aarush says.

The ride car seats two across. Aarush climbs in first, sliding over to the far seat. I really, really hate roller coasters, and my heart is pounding so hard in my chest I worry it's going to burst right out the top of my skull. But Aarush reaches out an arm and steadies me as I climb in beside him.

We both take our seats.

For a moment nothing happens. A long enough moment that I'm about to turn to Aarush and ask him if he thinks we're supposed to do something.

Then, like a house coming to life after a blackout, everything flares on all at once. Red lights flash and sparkle, and suddenly I can see the track ahead of us. The shoulder restraints come down on top of us with an echoing clang and a click.

We're stuck on the ride now, that's for sure.

Music with loud, crashing cymbals comes from the speakers in the headrests right behind us. It's so thundering and near, but with the thickly padded shoulder restraints, I can't reach my ears to cover them.

Then the music dims, and we hear a little boy's voice—a high, sped-up, frenzied voice like a kid who got into his mom's caffeine-spiked energy drink.

Hello, friends! Welcome! Welcome to the ride! Are you ready, friends? Are you ready to scream your head off? Are you ready to get the wind pulled from your lungs? Are you ready to wish you'd never been born?

I grip the handles on the shoulder restraints with all my might. The voice and the music suddenly stop. We wait, suspended in that silent, terrifying moment.

Then we take off. We accelerate so fast my head flies back against the headrest. The music blasts on again, ringing and piercing in my ears. I start to scream, but my breath really is tugged out of my lungs before I can make a sound. The cold air gusts right into my face. I can hardly inhale against the frigid whooshing of air in my mouth and eyes, not to mention the muscle-tensing terror keeping my arms and hands and lungs clenched tight. Everything in me wants this to *stop*, but it just goes faster and faster. Finally, I manage a couple of gasps, and by then we're zipping fast around corners, rattling in tight circles, and then climbing up and up a tall hill.

That's the loop, Aarush says, shouting over the music and the wind and the clanking of the track.

We slowly, slowly get higher and higher. The ground seems impossibly far below us, yet the track keeps on going, farther up into the empty sky. I want to close my eyes tight shut, but I'm more afraid of not seeing what's coming. The higher we get, the slower we seem to go, until finally, agonizingly, we reach the top of the hill.

Oh gosh oh gosh oh gosh. Now I can scream. We crest the top and start zooming zooming zooming down the other side. Both of us are screaming so loud we might lose our voices, and all my guts feel like they're levitating inside me. Then we hit the loop. That's when I do close my eyes, and it all goes by so fast, but I can feel my head swirling, feel the blood rushing into my skull and my sinuses, and feel the centrifugal force pushing me back into my seat as we circle upside down.

On the other side of the loop, I hear Aarush muttering, *Okay, okay,* to himself. The ride keeps going and going, lights streaking by as we pass. We fling around corners, bounce up and down, jostle in our seats. We drop down smaller hills that turn my guts into whirlpools again and again. We seem to pass back around nearer the fair lights.

Soon we're slowly going up another tall, looming hill.

Wait a second, Aarush yells. *Isn't this the same hill as before?*

It's hard to tell in the dark, but what I can see past the blinding neon lights looks possibly familiar. These lights, the steep hill, the particular shadows.

Maybe, yeah, I call back to Aarush.

I didn't see the loading dock, he says.

We hit the top of the hill again, zoom down, and are flung back up into the loop. This time I peek my eyes open, trying not to get too disoriented looking down at the track below us.

This time, as the ride keeps going and as my guts adjust to being tossed around like we're in a blender stuck on high,

I keep a lookout for the loading dock. I expected the ride to take us somewhere else—to the Fear Maker—but it seems like we're going in circles. We repeat the ride again, but it's as if the platform where we got on has just disappeared.

The ride keeps going and going.

We go up the hill again and again.

We're flung into the loop again and again.

Which means we're stuck.

Which means that the question now is: How do we get off?

What do we do? I yell to Aarush.

I don't know, he yells back.

The track curves around a corner, the force pushing my body to one side. When we straighten out, Aarush's hand reaches forward. The wind's in my eyes, but I see what he's reaching for. There's a small panel in front of us, a little latch I hadn't noticed before, with a tiny, doll-sized handle. It just looks like part of the mechanics of the ride. It takes a second through all the turning and bumping, but eventually, pinching the handle between two fingers, Aarush gets the latch open.

The panel swings on a hinge. Behind the door are two vertical slots, one on Aarush's side and one on mine. Between the two slots is a large gold coin, held securely in place by several small metal brackets. The coin is bigger than a silver dollar, and reflects all the lights as we pass. It's engraved with a skull and the words *The Fear Maker.*

We stare at the open compartment for a moment, the coin and the two slots, while we're flying around some more corners.

That's how we escape the ride, Aarush says.

He's right. I know he's right, but I don't want to admit it. I refuse to admit it, because—

There's only one coin, I say.

I can hardly see Aarush around our hefty restraints, but leaning forward I can just see his eyes and the top of his face down to his nose. He's leaning forward, too, looking back at me.

You can do this, Penny, he says.

No no no. The wind pulls the moisture from my eyes. We have to yell to be heard over the whipping air and the clanking metal. *I'm not going without you. That wasn't our plan. I can't go without you.*

Yes, you can, he says.

But I never would have made it this far, I say, my eyes stinging. *You got the bone-key. You picked door number seven. Even here, with this stupid coin thing, you're the one who figured out how to escape.*

And you saw through the fake parents, he shouts. *The fake fire, the fake food. You saw through the tricks.*

I'm shaking, and it's not just the roller coaster. I can't reach the sunflower seeds in my pocket. I can't quite remember the words in my grandma's best poem. Why did the Gardener think I had what I needed inside me, when all I can find is just fear and fear and more fear? I want more than anything to curl up and disappear.

Hey, Aarush says. I look at him. *You're Penny Hope. You can beat him.*

I gulp and it's like I'm swallowing down the entire night sky. This repulsive place was only survivable because I had my best friend, and now I have to finish this thing alone? Leave Aarush here? What if the Fear Maker wins and I'm never-endingly alone, a broken, petrified penny in the muck, and we're all stuck here forever and ever and ever?

But someone has to keep going. It's like the Gardener said: This is *my* monster. I don't know if Aarush is right about me, but I know I'm the one who has to do this. I brought Aarush here. I have to get him out. I have to get him and my parents and everyone else out.

I have to stand face-to-face with the Fear Maker.

It might be the only chance we've got.

We're at the bottom of the big hill, slowly making our way to the top. I've lost track of how many times we've gone around and around this thing. At least I won't be afraid of loop roller coasters anymore.

I reach out, my fingers barely able to touch the gold coin. I carefully lift it free of the brackets.

The coin glints in the neon light. It's cold, rimmed with grooved edges. We're nearing the top of the hill and I look at Aarush one last time. He nods.

My hands are shaking and my eyes are streaming tears that get wind-whipped from my cheeks as they fall. Somehow I manage to slip the gold coin into the slot on my side.

With a clink, I feel my shoulder restraints unlatch.

Now we're at the top of the hill.

Now, when I push, my shoulder restraints fling upward and I'm loose.

We rush, rush down the hill, toward the loop, and I am unhooked and unprotected.

And as we curve upside down, as we hit the top of the loop with the Fear Maker's world below us, I close my eyes and fall.

Falling Poem

I am falling, falling through endless
space, a forever rabbit hole.
Even while I fall,
even though I can't
tell if my eyes are open or closed,
I keep glimpsing things in my periphery.
Raining, clattering teeth, piling up.
An open book oozing blood.
My face in a mirror, utterly blank.
My dad hanging upside down, unmoving.
The corner-eye tricks keep coming
and I
just
keep
f
a
l
l
i
n
g.

Am I falling fast or slow?

I think about a lone astronaut
drifting away into space.
Then—is that ground
below? Ground coming up
fast and then everything
goes
black.

When I open my eyes
a man is standing over me.
His eyes glow red
and his teeth are pearly white.
I jump up. Screaming
will do no good.

The Fear Maker smiles.

Hello, Penny.

Penny Hope and the Fear Maker

The Fear Maker is nicely dressed.

He is in a tailored bloodred suit and tie, which match his glowing eyes. His hair is oily dark and slick, his shoes polished to perfection. His diamond cuff links flicker in the faint, pale light, the same color as his waxen face. He looks at me like a snake looks at a mouse, and his fancy put-togetherness makes me feel even more like he could beat me at any game I tried to play against him.

I back away from him until I hit a wall. I can't tell what kind of place this is, besides a deep, deep hole. The wall is too smooth to be earth and too earthy to be stone. Moonlight comes from a single opening high, high above us. It's not much light, but enough to tell that we're in some kind of pit or well, the Fear Maker and I.

I put my palms against the wall behind me, never taking my eyes off him, but pressed against the wall my backpack presses into my back and some part of me registers the hard edge of my notebook, that at least that made it here with me. It's cold and silent in this pit. There is only one door, and it is behind the Fear Maker.

Then the Fear Maker starts clapping. Slow. Sarcastic. Laughing.

Well, he says. *This has been a highly entertaining evening.*

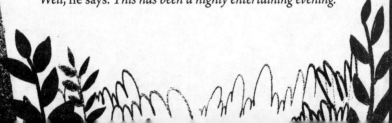

His voice is like crystal, like the clear slice of a sharpening knife, and all my defenses suddenly feel like nothing more than papier-mâché. I want to shrink. I want to curl in on myself until I disappear like those mouths in the wall.

In an instant, the Fear Maker shifts to anger. He steps toward me, his red eyes flashing. *You thought you could just come into my house, hmm? MY HOUSE?*

My knees are starting to buckle. I never should have left Aarush. How could I possibly have thought I could do this on my own?

You're as pathetic as your parents, the Fear Maker says, like I'm something he's trying to scrape off the bottom of his shoe. *I wish I could tell you that your parents were a satisfying meal, but their thin, flimsy little souls wouldn't fill a rat.*

He looks so human, this Fear Maker, with his shiny hair and suit, but it's as if all the human pieces don't add up to a whole. Inside what seems human are spikes and claws and malice. He's devoured my parents' souls. Any second he will devour me.

What a quaint dinner theater you've been, my dear, he says. *Ever since that Halloween. A sincere thank-you for your offering, by the way. Did you enjoy my little treat? Or do you like the tricks better? It's quite the playground you've let me into, my pet. And all these little plans of yours, these feeble attempts to fight me, they've been absolutely scrumptious. Such a delicious morsel. Now even your precious Gardener has left you for the worthless penny you are. You realize that by now, surely?*

He steps closer, his white teeth gleaming. *You thought you could fight me all by yourself? You thought you could change the ending of this nightmare? I was always going to eat you whole.*

He laughs and laughs, and the echoes are loud. *Have you ever done anything right in your life?* he says.

This is it, I think. I lost. I can't inhale. My vision is blurred.

This is the end.

My stomach feels like a vacuum.

I curl over myself.

And when I do, I feel the seeds in my pocket pressing against my leg.

I manage to get my trembling fingers into my pocket. My knuckles rub against the denim.

The seeds are still there. Still there.

I'll always be right here, the Gardener said. *I'm not going anywhere.*

Somehow, somehow, my hand clenches around those seeds like a lifeline, and I stand up straight.

The Fear Maker sneers at me.

Even as he steps toward me, he's still standing in front of the door. Angling himself between me and my way out, like he's guarding it. There are several yards between us, but it still feels like he is taking up the whole space, looming over me. The door behind him is wood, simple, but exquisitely carved and polished, with a wrought-iron knob.

With everything I've got I hold on to my seeds.

It takes several seconds to get my voice to work, but eventually I manage it.

Your . . . I clear my throat. *Your heart is in there, isn't it?* I say. *That's where the trapped souls . . . where my parents are.*

He laughs again. Do his teeth look sharper?

Oh, you are truly a delightful little toy, aren't you? It is just delectable how hard you try. His eyes flare. *Of course it's not. Oh, my sweet.*

The seeds press into my palms, each one something Grandma or the Gardener said that is finally clicking in my brain, finally starting to make sense. I think of the nights of Grandma reading to me. How she asked, what if I'm more powerful than this monster? I think of the Gardener's voice. He destroys and distorts, the Gardener said, but he can't create. I think of the fake parents here in this maze, made of tricks and illusions. I think of the fake fire and the fake fair and the rooms made of lies and traps.

A feast of the unreal.

The seeds tight in my grip are real.

I have more power, Grandma said. He can't create like I can, the Gardener said.

And there, hunched in that hole with the Fear Maker, I think I finally, finally get what they've been saying.

The Gardener said that when I needed it most, when I was at the most desperate limits, I would find the Garden.

I think I just did.

Because the Gardener never abandoned me.

The Fear Maker is lying.

Everything he says is a lie.

I cling to the true things, like the seeds in my pocket. Mom and Dad, the real ones, my original triangle family. Aarush, who came with me even though it hurt. Grandma and her poems, her open arms. And the Garden's yellow light, the Gardener's warmth and earthy smell and bright, bright flowers, shining from the inside. Holding on to that, like hope, is like trying to catch mist, but I cling to those sunflower-seed thoughts.

And when I step forward, the Fear Maker steps back.

My grandma told me I have more power than you can even imagine, I say.

The Fear Maker's eyes narrow. It's like my wrists had been tied, and the Gardener's and Grandma's words have finally cut through the knots, setting me free.

I step forward again.

The Gardener said I already have everything I need to beat you.

Now the Fear Maker looks livid. Ready to spit poison. And in fact, a reptilian forked tongue flickers between his teeth, which now look like fangs. He hisses, and the sound echoes up the chamber walls.

I step forward again.

The Gardener never left. That's a lie. Everything you just told me is a lie. About that door, about my parents' souls. My swallowed sobs have opened up the way for roaring, for shouting my voice full force, and I do. I'm not the mouse anymore. I am the lion.

And about me. You're lying about me. I'm not nothing. But this place is. This whole place is a lie. None of this is real. It's all a facade. Smoke and mirrors. You distort and twist and warp, but you don't create anything of your own. In fact, I don't think you can.

Now he is fully transformed and writhing. He is monstrous. He is all spikes and pale, wormy flesh. He is fangs and claws and sinuous muscle. He is human and wolf and serpent all at once. He moves the way nightmares move, in waves and jump cuts, but in some ways it's a relief to see him in his true form, to see exactly who I'm fighting, no more tricks, no more wondering what's really hiding under the bed. He towers over me and lets out a gut-deep screech that seems to ring from eons and eons ago. Rings all through my bones.

But he's too late.

Because I finally know what my grandma and the Gardener were telling me all along.

I look into his flashing red eyes.

"You're no maker," I say. "But I am."

And I throw one of my sunflower seeds into his open, gaping mouth.

His screeching stops. He freezes. His eyes are open wide, suspended in that moment as if all the air was suddenly sucked out of the room.

In that quick second, he looks at me once more. His eyes are focused, like he's actually seeing me for the first time. There's shock there, on his face. Then a grimace. A contorted sneer like an opossum caught in daylight.

The frozen moment ends. Then it's as if he's burning from the inside out. His pale, pasty flesh cracks with writhing flame and molten lava beneath it. His screech becomes a howl. A howl that might once have terrified me, but now, at least for a moment, I know what I am, and what I am is more powerful than him. I hear his screeching howl for what it really is. Not a howl of power or even pain, but a howl of unfulfilled greed. A howl of spoiled, frustrated malice. The sound of a petulant child throwing a tantrum.

More and more of him becomes ash. His body of tricks and deceit couldn't handle something as real as a sunflower seed, and the burning works its way through. Then even the ash is gone, after the fire has consumed him. Only a few last whiffs of smoke billowing up through the opening above, into the night sky, like the last echoes of his raging wail.

I exhale, and something in me is released. The rotten apple seed that's lived in my gut for so long feels obliterated, disintegrated, the same way my sunflower seed disintegrated the monster. When I breathe out, it's as if that breath is the last remnants of that seed following the smoke up and out into the sky. I feel light, like I am finally right in my body for the first time in a long, long time.

And then I am alone.

Just me, Penny Hope, with my empty notebook and my sunflower seeds.

Everything is still, and so quiet, not a quiet of waiting monsters, but one of peace and steady, calm waters. After that deafening inferno, I want to sit in that stillness for a moment, like a balm. It's going to take a while to wrap my head around what just happened. I feel both new and familiar to myself, like I'm waking up.

There are those documentaries they show on the National Geographic channel sometimes, about grasslands or woods being scorched away by huge forest fires, leaving nothing but ash and devastated earth. But then they show what happens next—the tiny blades of green poking through the dirt. A seed, freshly cracked open, with a vibrant little stem shooting upward.

That's what I feel like.

Cracked open, my soul shooting upward.

The trills of smoke drift into the sky. I don't think the Fear Maker is gone for good. I still glimpse some of the smoke he left behind at the corner of my eye, like it's waiting to catch me unawares. Waiting to blind me. But right now, my eyes are clear, and there's a door ahead of me that needs opening.

Heart Tree

The door in the pit—
the door to the fearmonger's heart—
opens
because I tell it to.
<u>Let me through,</u> I say,
and it does, opening into a
small room, square, oozing
thick gunk like tar
and reflective oil—blood
of nightmares, covering
the floor inches deep.
Right at the center, a column
of the slick ooze,
towering up to the ceiling
like the trunk of a rotted tree.
Black tendrils vine
and twist like branches
or veins overhead.
This room, a sickly, dead atria.
A place where things come to die—
a garden upside down.
I take slow, sticky steps
around the room
around the column-tree-aorta.

Step, step, because if I don't
keep moving
the oozing ground begins to pull me
under
sinking me like sticky quicksand.
This time, though, I know
what fear is, and his leftover
bag of fake tricks
can't stop me.
Up to the trunk I step, reaching
out my finger. The tree, too,
tugs, tries to suck me in.
My mom and dad—
the real ones—
here somewhere.
I know it like sunlight,
like a breeze.
They're trapped in the muck,
the goo. But if I dive in
I'll be stuck, too.
What I need is something to break
through this oily, oozing,
lifeless ground,
something with roots
stronger than a fearmonger's heart.
Something bright enough to burn away
oppressive clouds, something hardier
than nightmares.

Something like a handful of sunflower seeds.
I don't know if I'll ever
find the Garden again
but I think of my parents
and take every seed from my pocket
and one by one
I press each seed
into rotted earth.
Seed after seed, until the last,
and I don't wait long
for change.
The ground under my feet
hardens. Ooze freezes,
uneven ripples and hills.
Then
    CRACK
like breaking eggshells,
life cracking
its way out
into the open.
Cracks splitting
all across the floor.
There is starlight
in the cracks,
the whole ground sparkling.
The center trunk swirls
with starlight glimmer.
Then a hand

pushing through, cracking the earth
like young shoots, new growth.
This hand, one I know
as well as my own,
carefully painted nails,
a mole on the ring finger.
A hand I'd know anywhere.
And I run
run
my ground-cracking steps
leaving prints of starlight.
I grab the hand with mine
and pull, pull, pull,
with every ounce of strength
I have left.
Tug, pull, tug, pull
and finally
my mom is standing there—
really there, real as earth—
next to me
looking dazed.
My arms fling around her
before I can blink,
wrapped so tight,
squeezing-air-from-lungs tight
because she's here.
She's back, a sunrise,
a new day returning.

Penny? she says.
Words, sometimes, are
too small, so I just
hold her tighter
and she holds me
right back.
Until there's another hand,
and I know this one, too.
Reach, pull, tug.
I'm watering the underground
stars with laughing tears,
exhausted, laughing tears,
because I have my parents back.
My real
every-part-of-them
parents back.
My dad wraps all of us
into a bouquet
and now, tucked
like a fresh sunflower
where I belong,
I can, for the first time
since the nightmares began,
breathe.
The walls of the pit and the house
have disappeared
crumbled like spent firewood

prison walls tumbling down
and we're outside
outside
where there are
so many stars
the Milky Way bright enough
to drink.
An owl calls, <u>whoooo</u>
and I see more people
the baker
Gladys in her pink scrubs
Mr. Reitman
cautious-stepping, blinking
like they just woke up.
And there, in moonlight,
Aarush
effervescent
and sandwiched tight
between his parents.
Smiling, his eyes brimming starlight,
he nods at me and waves,
a slow wave,
incandescently happy to be safe
and utterly worn down by
what we went through.
I wave back.
Wave the million and one things

we don't know how to say.
Then all the ooze is gone,
every drop, leaving only
rich, grassy earth.
And in the center,
where the fearmonger's heart
rose high, no longer
a column of muck,
but a cluster of tall, golden
sunflowers.
I don't care if I'm too old,
I take my mom's and dad's hands.
Dazed, they
smile down at me.
Let's go home, I say.
I lead them
out of the clearing,
where the creaking, hungry house
no longer stands.
I lead and Aarush is right behind
and all the other lost souls follow
back through the trees
back to the streetlamps and houses
and everyone says a sleepy good night
and finds home.
Mom and Dad and I make it inside.
We head to our rooms.
Before I close my door, Mom says,

Want to make
orange rolls tomorrow?
Yeah. I say. Let's
make
lots and lots.

A Few Weeks Later

Just put the big bowl by the sink, Mom says. *I'll wash it later.*

I carry the serving bowl that's been emptied of its mashed potatoes and set it on the counter. Dad's already loaded most of the smaller dishes into the dishwasher. I hurry back to the living room before Aarush and his family say goodbye.

Tonight, we're celebrating. Mom got a job as a manager for a little bookstore downtown. She said it's not what she expected, and is going to take a lot of work, but when she said it, her eyes sparkled like an exciting new dream was reflecting in them. Aarush and his family came over, and Grandma came, too. Over a basket of orange rolls, she asked me her new usual question. Whispered. A secret between us.

Any sign of the monster?

I gave her my usual response.

Smoke, but no fire.

That's my girl, Grandma said, lightly tugging my braid.

I'm working on some new poems, one of them maybe called "Smoke but No Fire." I hope it will be better than any of the poems I lost to the mouths in the house in the woods.

I'm also working on a poem for the contest, and it's almost ready. It's a sonnet like the one Grandma loves. But I've gone as far as I can with it and don't know how to fix it. It needs someone else's eyes. Which means I have to show my words,

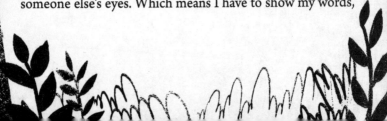

the words from the deepest inside parts of me, and let someone else look at them. I'm scared.

Dad's in the driveway, ready to drive Grandma home. The Banerjees wait by the front door, saying goodbye. Aarush's little brother jumps up and down on their dad's feet.

Nobody but Aarush and I remembers the house in the woods, or much of anything about that night. Our souls were never stolen, after all. Everyone went home and slept the deepest sleep of their lives, and the next morning, Mom's eyes were still that foresty green, and everyone did what they normally do. Mom and I bought cupcakes from the bakery, and the baker's hazel eyes were bright and happy. At the assisted living home, I walked around until I found Gladys, and when I saw her blue eyes looking at something on the computer screen, I almost wanted to run up and give her a hug and cry with relief. I couldn't even be mad when Mr. Reitman sent a girl to the principal's office for chewing gum.

Grandma remembers me calling her that night. Remembers to ask about the monsters every time she sees me, just in case.

I run out to the driveway and tap on the passenger window. Grandma rolls it down.

Grandma? I gulp. *I've been working on a poem. A sonnet, kind of based off the one you said was your favorite. This is the one I want to use for that contest with Aarush. Would you ... would it be all right if you helped me with it?*

Grandma smiles and claps her hands like she's never been so excited. I've never been brave enough to ask for help with one of my poems before, but I figure Grandma is a good place to start.

Oh, lucky Penny, of course! she says. *I'd be honored.*

Dad winks, and he and Grandma back out of the driveway.

I think about her words and the Gardener's words helping me through that maze of fear. I wouldn't have made it without their help. Maybe that's why a triangle is the strongest shape—all the sides leaning securely against one another.

I even told my mom about some of my nightmares, and she had an awesome idea. We're going to paint nightmare pillowcases. Then, I thought, if the nightmares come back, I can paint the nightmares on rocks and tie them up inside the pillowcase, the way zoologists do with venomous snakes. Mom might not remember the haunted house, but I think she has some very smart strategies to fight any monsters yet to come.

Aarush remembers. He remembers everything. He says he was on that roller-coaster ride for a long, long time. He looped and looped until he blacked out and woke up in the clearing.

And he remembers to ask me whether I've seen the Gardener again. I always tell him no, I haven't, but I'm still looking. And I am. I always will be.

For now, I'm back in the front entry, saying goodbye to my best friend, and I hold my hand up in front of my face, fingers splayed and wiggling. He does the same, a grin revealing his deep dimples.

We have a secret handshake now.

Bone, he says.

Flames, I say.

And we high-five.

You guys are weird, Mom says, in a way that says how glad she is about that.

Later that night, Mom and Dad and I watch *Babe*—my new favorite movie—and Dad keeps making pig snort noises. Afterward, when I'm walking up the stairs to bed, I turn around and say, *Hey, Dad, what's your favorite flower?*

He leans back on the couch with his hands behind his head. *Hmm. I think right now it's night-blooming jasmine. How cool is it that some flowers only bloom at night? Plus, they smell incredible.*

I want to say, *I'm so glad you're back.* I want to tell them both that I'd do it all again. I settle for, *Good one, Dad.*

How about you? he says.

I smile like I'm keeping a secret, which, maybe I am. *Sunflowers*, I say.

Almost as bright as you, he says.

I walk slowly up the stairs to my room, thinking about all the poems and gardens and sweet treats I want to make.

And when I get upstairs, my bedroom door is glowing.

The Way Here

He's waiting for me with arms open.

"You did great," he says, his voice rough and choked with emotion. I bury my face in his big brown coat. "You did so great, Penny Hope."

His hug is so safe. There's my breathable sky. The humming flowers.

"Oh man, I missed this place," I say. "I missed it so much."

"Just takes a penny's worth of hope to get here." The Gardener winks.

"You sound like my grandma."

"Smart woman."

We walk and we walk. I feel my skin soaking in the breeze and the yellow and wonder if this is what photosynthesis feels like.

"I told him he was just a fearmonger," I say. "Not a maker of anything."

The Gardener nods. "That's right."

"What if he comes back?" I ask.

The Gardener nods again. "He's greedy. And a very sore loser."

Step step step. "But I'm Penny Hope," I say.

When the Gardener smiles, it's even warmer than the photosynthesis on my skin. "But you're Penny Hope," the Gardener agrees.

I think of the smoke drifting up from the fearmonger's

ashes. Smoke waiting in the shadows under the trees. Waiting to re-form, waiting at the corner of my eye, waiting to catch me unawares and to seep in and cloud my thoughts.

If I could just get back here, to this Garden, when I need it . . .

"When will I see you again?" I ask. The constant question. "This place. When you say a penny's worth of hope . . . I thought it was desperation, but . . . is there an easier way to get back here?"

We've passed our bench, strolled through the tallest flowers, and reached the little cottage. The Gardener looks at me, waiting for me to answer my own question.

I think back through everything. The blank eyes. The house in the woods. The bones and fire. The oozing, unalive, oily tar tree. That room of the fearmonger's heart.

How could he compare with this place? How could any of his illusions compete with the reality of *here*?

They couldn't. He couldn't.

I have an answer. One of many, perhaps.

The flowers themselves seem to lean in when I talk.

"Is this place . . . this Garden . . . I've felt like it was making me stronger from the inside. Is that true? Is this Garden really outside of me, or is it . . . inside? Is it a real garden? Is it my heart-room the way the ooze tree was his?"

The Gardener doesn't answer. Maybe the answer is both: inside *and* outside. He quietly grins, takes my hands in his, and gives me two more handfuls of sunflower seeds to always carry with me.

My Monster's Eyes Are Nothing: My Sonnet 130

My monster's eyes are nothing like the sun.
Blood is far less red than his eyes glow red.
His soulless grasping no one can outrun.
If living skin is vivid, his is dead.
Be ready—life and joy he will entomb.
There's only malice when my monster speaks.
I'd rather smell corpse flowers in full bloom
than all the rotting scents my monster reeks.
All things sweet, he'll change their taste to sour.
He'll spin you till you don't know where to go.
All the nightmares', demons', monsters' power
is behind him. Oh yes, your fear's his show.
And yet, for utter triumph all you need
are allied hearts and the hope inside one seed.

Acknowledgments

When I was little, I read Roald Dahl's *The Witches* probably fifty times. I loved the eeriness, the feeling of covert creepy eking out into the real world, which meant you could fight it. I loved the unassuming child hero and the adult who took them absolutely seriously.

When I was little, I had a recurring nightmare character. He chased me around playgrounds and dark hallways. I remember, in my nightmare, trying to hide or pretending to sleep. (If I was asleep, he couldn't get me. That was the rule.) I remember cracking open my dream eyelids to check if he was still there and seeing his wide, staring eyes inches from mine.

That is the ground on which *The Nightmare House* was grown, but as with any book, it took many, many gardeners to make.

Thanks, first and always, to my mom and dad for being the place I went after those nightmares. And for everything, everything else. Thank you to my grandparents; the sunflower roots run deep.

Thank you to my incredible, superpowered, and limitlessly savvy agent, Rena Rossner. You are the perfect shepherd for my weird self and all my weird stories told in weird ways. My writing horizons are so much broader with you on my team. Thank you to Melissa Warten for saying okay when I brought you this quirky nightmare of a book that was so different from what I'd done before and for making it so much more vivid and powerful than I could have dreamed. Thank you to Wes Adams for taking this on and picking it up so considerately and thoughtfully, and to Hannah Miller, Shyamala Parthasarathy, Allyson Floridia, Chandra Wohleber, Celeste Cass, and everyone else who helped turn this odd story into a book. Including and importantly, designer Mallory Grigg and illustrator Angie Hewitt, whose pitch-perfect artwork made me gasp when I first saw it—and still does.

Karley, my soul sister, thank you for coming into my life at exactly the right time and for letting me show you *Sense and Sensibility* at two a.m. Kim, thank you for being both my rock and my magic feather and for your wisdom both in writing and in life. Dianna, thank you for being the miracle place I landed for a while and for all the goodness you put into the world. Amanda, thank you for offering your throat to the wolf with the red roses—you didn't do anything wrong. Thank you to Amanda Rawson Hill, Cindy Baldwin, Celesta Rimington, Arianne Costner, Jenny Esplin, Jess Hernandez, Ellie Terry, all my wonderful Mighty Middle Grade friends, and so, so many others for your writing mentorship, commiseration, and wisdom. I could not do this without you. Thank you to Jessica, Roommate, Kaitlin, Kinner, Bobbi Sue, Elise, Amanda, Tiffany, Jenessa, Madeleine, Allison, Tesia, Nikki, Jordan, John, Mr. K, and many others for the desperately needed cheerleading and support now and for many years.

Lastly, to you, dear reader. If you're fighting a Fear Maker, and we all are, remember the light. Remember the light and the sunflower gardens and the real Maker of all good things. He made you and the Gardeners on both sides of the veil, who are there to help you. Fear is no Maker, but *you* are. And compared to the blazing fire of you, fear is just ash in the wind.